Night Call

& Other Stories

Tales of Murder and Mystery

Pauline Kirk + Jo Summers
(P J Quinn)

PJ QUINN

© PJ Quinn 2024

All rights reserved. No part of this book may be reproduced or distributed in any form without prior written permission from the authors, with the exception of non-commercial uses permitted by copyright law. No part of this book may be reproduced or transmitted by any means, except as permitted by UK copyright law or the authors. For licensing requests, please contact the authors at www.fightingcockpress.co.uk

The story, all names, characters, and incidents portrayed in this production are fictitious. No identification with actual persons (living or deceased), places, buildings, and products is intended or should be inferred.

Published by Fighting Cock Press
2 Pinfold Close
Riccall
York YO19 6QZ

ISBN: 978-0-906744-46-8

Book cover designed by Piers Schofield.

Also by PJ Quinn:

The D I Ambrose Mysteries,
published by Stairwell Books

Foul Play
Poison Pen
Close Disharmony
Poetic Justice
Skull Days

By Pauline Kirk

Waters of Time,
Century Hutchinson, reissued by Stairwell Books

The Keepers,
Virago/Little Brown, reissued by Stairwell Books

Border 7,
Stairwell Books
Available on Audible (read by author)

www.stairwellbooks.co.uk
www.pjquinn.co.uk
www.paulinemkirk.co.uk

PJ Quinn

PJ Quinn is the pen name of mother and daughter team, Pauline Kirk and Jo Summers.

Pauline is a published novelist and poet. Jo is a lawyer and writes textbooks and articles for the legal press.

Jo challenged her mother to write a crime novel, and somehow, ended up writing with her. The result, so far, is a series of five detective novels, the DI Ambrose Mysteries, set in the late 1950's and early 1960's.

They have also written short stories which have been published in a wide range of journals and broadcast on local radio. Eighteen of these stories, sharing the themes of mystery or murder, have been collected here.

With thanks to Helen, Nicky and Pippa

Contents

The Devil's Hand 1
Night Call 9
The Dream Machine 13
Harald's Yard 21
Jardinière 30
Etcetera 41
Apple Blossom 50
Sophie's Choice 53
Safe House 58
The Bread Man 61
Cavern 73
Tie a Red Ribbon 80
The Deadly Morris Dance 93
For The Children 102
Glebe House 116
The Tennis Girls 124
Bandstand 131
The Rains 145
Poetic Justice 156
Acknowledgements 161

The Devil's Hand

"Surely, Reverend, you don't believe in ghosts?"

Malcolm's laughter gave way to silence. The Local History Group looked at the Vicar in surprise.

At first the clergyman didn't reply. He walked to the window and looked towards the spire of his church, nestling between two huge oak trees.

Finally, the Vicar turned to the group. "I should warn you off this line of research," he started, "but to do so would give way to superstition and rumour. Just keep an open mind and be very careful. You could open a box of secrets that should remain shut."

David opened his mouth to interject, but the Vicar continued. "Your starting point might as well be the grave. If you follow me, I'll show you where it is. It's still light enough."

Puzzled, the group followed the Vicar, hurrying behind him like parishioners late for mass. They entered the graveyard, turning right into the furthest corner. The graves here were the oldest. Stone lions kept silent guard. Frozen cherubim stared towards wilted roses.

Someone had tied a purple ribbon round an old white cross.

Passing a large angel on a marble plinth, the Vicar turned towards the wall. There, almost hidden, the group found a small grave, mottled grey and green.

"If you don't mind, I'll leave you here," the Vicar turned away. "I suggest you don't stay too long. It will be dark soon."

"And I'd advise you not to touch the grave," he added. "Strange things happen to those who do." A couple of the group shuddered as they watched him go.

"That's odd, don't you think?" It was David who spoke first. "This grave looks ancient, but the date seems to be 1919."

"Perhaps it's 1819?" Rebecca said.

"No, the dates are definitely 1895 to 1919," Gerry replied. "He wasn't very old when he died."

"What was he called?" Sally pushed forwards for a closer look.

"Presumably," Rita pointed out, "he was called Villiers. After all, Villiers Park was named after him."

"It's not what the grave says," Malcolm swallowed slightly. "I'd swear it says: 'Sir Joseph Devil'!"

He bent down for a better look. Forgetting the Vicar's warning, Malcolm ran his fingers over the withered stone. He was surprised at how warm and enticing it felt. Suddenly he jumped as he felt a heavy hand on his right shoulder. He glanced over but there was no one there. Shrugging, Malcolm looked back at the grave.

"It seems to have been changed at some point," he

said. "It looks like someone's added the letters 'D' and 'e' at the beginning and tried to scrub off the 'liers' at the end. Now why on earth would someone do that?" Malcolm raised his head to look at the others.

"Maybe," Rebecca replied quietly, "someone was trying to make a point?"

...

"That's it, just take it slowly," Kathy held her father's arm gently. She paused to let him catch his breath.

She'd been taking him for his walk for nearly a year now, ever since his stroke: since he'd no longer been able to walk alone or, for that matter, to choose where to go each afternoon. Villiers Park, opposite the nursing home, was perfect: easy to get to, with plenty of benches for her father to rest on.

They took their usual route, past the tennis courts to the ornamental pond. Then they stopped, as they did every day, to look at the small golden fish. In spring they'd seen tadpoles and later watched the tiny frogs hopping away.

Kathy turned but was surprised when her father didn't move. He was still staring at the pond. She followed his gaze, straining her eyes to see if he'd spotted one of the little newts that skulked along the bottom. The still water reflected the sky above, the clouds skidding across the surface. Then Kathy saw the water-sky darken, the clouds growing in size, an ominous green-black. Another face suddenly appeared, mirrored right next to hers: an oval face, pale and female. The woman was crying.

Kathy was puzzled. She hadn't heard the woman approach, or her sobbing.

Looking up, Kathy found herself staring into thin air. Perplexed, she turned back to her father, but he was still staring at the pond. Glancing back at the water, she saw again the reflection of the sad, weeping lady; except the only person near was her father.

Kathy was silent as she took her father home.

...

It was a whim that brought her out again to the park. She knew where her feet were taking her before she even got to the pond. Kathy leant against the railings, scrutinising the water carefully. She was certain her mind must have been playing tricks. She could hardly ask her father what he'd seen. Even if he hadn't lost the power of speech, he would have probably made no sense. He'd had early-stage dementia even before the stroke.

Kathy had no problem believing in the supernatural. She'd listened to friends' stories of ghostly sightings with regret. She'd hoped one day she might see for herself whether spirits did exist. It made her feel better to think that her father's soul might still be intact, within the barely functioning physical host.

She had been daydreaming for some time, staring intently at the pond. She hadn't even noticed the face appear next to hers.

Kathy came to with a start. There was absolutely no doubt that she was looking at another woman's mirror-face, right next to hers. The woman had stopped sobbing, but tears still streaked her cheeks. Kathy didn't need turn her head to know that she was alone at the pond. She tried to remain calm. On an impulse, she spoke to the reflection. It seemed the right thing to do. Of course, she realised that anyone seeing her would have thought her mad: staring at the water, talking to herself. She also realised she had absolutely no idea what to say to a ghost.

She finally decided on a simple "Hello". The pale reflection turned its head to acknowledge her.

Astonished, Kathy tried again. "Is there anything I can do to help?" This time the head shook.

Again, Kathy ran out of things to say. Finally, she asked "are you going to be alright if I leave you?"

The reflection paused. There was a slight shrug of the shoulders. Kathy realised she could now see more of the woman. She was dressed in white muslin, like an old-fashioned summer dress; the type Kathy's grandmother would have worn as a girl. The woman was young and beautiful. She wore her blond hair up away from her face, flattering her delicate cheekbones. Kathy was suddenly struck by their likeness. She could have been looking at her much younger, prettier sister. It was no wonder her father had been so confused.

As Kathy stared at the reflection, a hand appeared at its neck: a male hand, gloved and large. The hand disappeared but Kathy understood. The lady had been strangled.

"Oh my God!" Kathy couldn't help it; the words tumbled out. "Did they catch who did this to you?"

The woman shook her head. "But do you know who he was?" Kathy was insistent. The woman nodded, starting to cry again.

"There must be something I can do to help. I can try to make sure he's punished," Kathy exclaimed.

"Don't worry," a male voice said behind her. "He'll probably be punished for eternity."

Wheeling round, Kathy came face to face with the Vicar. "I see you've met Ellen," he added.

...

"So, what makes you so sure?" David asked as they walked through the park. It had been raining heavily; the ground was soft beneath their feet. A flock of seagulls was trying to out-screech the crows.

"Sir Joseph Villiers was injured in the Great War," Malcolm replied. "When he got back his fiancée, Ellen Longbottom, disappeared. I think Joseph killed her and then committed suicide. Either that or he was lynched by the local mob for her murder. He was so hot-tempered, he was known locally as 'The Devil' even before the War."

"He was probably suffering shell shock," David said. "But she may just have left him. You can't be certain he killed her."

They were walking down a tree-lined path, towards old Villiers Hall. Despite being turned into tiny flats, the building was still beautiful. Malcolm stopped in the shade of two ancient chestnut trees, their gnarled bark covered in green lichen.

"This is the oldest part of the park," Malcolm dropped his voice. He wasn't sure why he was whispering.

He found himself walking towards another tree, so large its trunk had split in two. Both sides twisted upwards, supported by wooden stakes. He saw with surprise that absolutely nothing was growing beneath: the ground was a barren brown. One of the wooden supports had pulled out of the ground. The soft earth seemed to have lost its hold. Stepping forward, Malcolm glanced down. He immediately wished he hadn't. A flash of white caught his eye. He was looking at a skull.

"How the hell did you know she was buried here?" David whistled quietly in astonishment.

Malcolm flushed slightly. He couldn't explain what had happened last night. How he'd not just visualised strangling the young lady, how he actually felt himself doing it. How he'd watched from above as he buried her body under a tree. Or how he'd woken in a sweat just as the noose was tightening around his neck. "I had a dream," was all he said.

...

Kathy stood in the graveyard, looking at the tombstone she'd just paid for. It simply stated "RIP, found at last." She had wanted to add Ellen's name, but the Vicar pointed out they couldn't be sure the skeleton was hers.

He had queried Kathy's other request too; that Ellen's ashes be placed near the body of her former fiancé. It was a strange choice, the Vicar felt, but finally he'd agreed. He wasn't sure Kathy was right, though, that putting them together would lay their ghosts to rest.

"I wonder if you can forgive a man, in death, who took your life?" Kathy mused out loud.

"Let's hope so," the Vicar replied. "I think they both deserve to lie in peace."

Kathy smiled, putting a hand out to touch the new gravestone. She was surprised how warm it felt yet a shiver went down her spine. Suddenly she felt dizzy and lightheaded. As she held on to the grave tightly for support, she felt a small, dainty hand on her shoulder.

"Are you alright, Kathy?" the Vicar sounded concerned.

She turned to look at him in surprise. "Why do you call me Kathy?" she asked. "My name's Ellen."

Night Call

"You're rubbish!"

In amazement I stared at the phone. "Who's there?" I asked.

"Someone who writes a lot better than you."

I expected to hear Mum was dying. Instead, some nutter was saying my play was no good. I would have slammed the phone down, but the voice was vaguely familiar.

"Who are you?" I persisted.

There was no reply, just laughter. It sounded bitter. We played a grotesque game, waiting to see who would speak first.

Finally, the voice began again. "Wouldn't you like to know?" it asked. I could hear music in the background, and muffled giggling, adult giggling. That was more unnerving than threats.

"You think you're so clever," the voice continued. "Standing there, talking drivel about how the cast had done it all. You couldn't construct a brick wall."

The speaker had been at the first night. They knew me. From their tone, they were not rational. I began to feel scared. My number was ex-directory. They probably knew where I lived.

I tried persuasion. They could be a writer themselves, jealous at my success, if you can call a five-day run at the local Rep success.

"The theatre's so unpredictable," I replied. "Your best work gets nowhere, and the silly sketch runs for weeks. One of yours will make it sometime. You're pretty good."

"You bet I am! But I don't sleep around."

"Nor do I," I said coldly.

There was definitely a Canadian accent, but I didn't know anyone from Canada. Presumably my tormentor could act. I thought I could hear a male voice in the background. It seemed to be saying, 'Give it up!'

"Try sending your work to John Kennet at the Rep," I suggested. "He's looking for talent."

It was the wrong thing. There was an explosion of foul air at the other end. I slammed the phone down.

It rang again, five minutes later. For a long time, I tried to ignore it, but Dad could be calling. As carefully as if I was handling a scorpion, I picked up the handset.

"Not asleep yet?" the voice asked. "Writing another masterpiece?"

"Get lost!" I shouted.

It was impossible to sleep now, but I lay down and tried. Then I thought of the answerphone. If I put that on, Dad, or the hospital, could contact me. Recording an insult would feel silly.

The answerphone wasn't working. I had forgotten. I was going to get myself a new phone, one of those modern ones that showed the caller's number. If I'd got round to it, I'd know who was plaguing me now. Cursing my stupidity, I went back to bed.

It was nearly an hour before the phone rang again, and for every minute my nerves were waiting.

The voice was definitely more slurred. "I tried sending stuff to John," it said, unannounced. "He sent it back. Didn't even include a note." There was no music now, or male voice. The speaker seemed to be alone. "But then I don't have your 'special relationship'," she added suddenly.

I still couldn't work out who was speaking. My dressing gown was too thin for a winter's night, and I was shivering. "I don't have any special relationship," I said, only to feel angry with myself. "It wouldn't be your business if I did," I added.

It sounded so lame. Furiously I put down the phone.

There were no more calls until six o'clock. Perhaps my night caller had fallen asleep, dead drunk or recovering from whatever high she favoured. I began to feel sorry for her.

Compassion evaporated when I got the last call. "I'm doing myself in, you know," the voice said, quite calmly. "Topping myself. It'll be your fault." Then the line went dead.

For a full minute I stared in horror. Then I tried to walk away. It was the ultimate bullying threat, the "You'll be sorry" technique. The trouble was: it could be true.

Shivering in the hall, I stared at the phone, willing it to ring. Nothing happened.

Finally, my mind cleared. My phone should let me redial the last number. My mind was too stupid with sleep and emotion to remember how to do it. I had to fumble through the phone buttons until I found it.

As soon as the number came up, I understood.

Urgently I dialled, but there was no answer. Putting the phone down, I tried to think what to do. By the time I'd driven round there, it could be too late. Magda was not the sort to make threats lightly, even when she was on the vodka and coke.

I doubt if she appreciated me sending an ambulance, but then, what are colleagues for?

The Dream Machine

"Just sit down dear," the nurse said. Esther sat, feeling high and vulnerable, while the receptionist closed the door. Two rows of buttons and indicator windows were set into the arms of the chair and a large screen was mounted round the walls. A trolley with the usual kidney shaped dishes and blood-pressure gauge stood by the window. The nurse smiled, pulling the blind down with a sharp crack. "Esther Thomas?" she asked. Carefully she checked the details on her board. "Number 58197/z/f? You're only here for a routine examination aren't you?"

"Yes. It's a bit unnerving all the same - I can't help but worry about the children too..."

"That's only natural," the nurse replied, tipping the chair backwards. "But the kiddies will be enjoying themselves. There's lots of toys in the crèche - we bought a new stimulator only the other week."

The chair was soft and cushioned, like a bed slightly raised, but Esther wouldn't close her eyes and rest, though her head was aching. The cafeteria had been closed, as it always was, a polite notice apologising for the inconvenience and hoping they had a nice day. The form filling had taken hours too. The waiting room had been comfortable of course, with a video set in the corner and piles of brightly coloured cushions scattered about the floor, but the time had dragged, while everyone whispered nervously without knowing why they were afraid. It was like being choked by an expensive, comfortable fur coat.

The nurse explained the details of the equipment. Basically, it was an adaptation of the stimulators provided for relaxation centres: a series of images would be thrown on the screen (rather like the old movies of the 1990's), and the patient could control their speed and content by pressing the appropriate knobs on the console. It was perfectly safe - quite pleasant really. The dream machines in provincial clinics were every bit as reliable as those in the Capital. Why, a government inspector tested the console every week. If her mind was clean and healthy, she need have nothing to fear.

Esther listened, smiling occasionally in agreement, as she'd been taught. She must concentrate on anger instead of fear. If that stupid woman hadn't quarrelled with her neighbour, there would have been no malicious reports to the local Keeper, no vetting of contacts, and she herself wouldn't have been brought in for reassessment. It was not her error, or even that of another member of the movement which had brought her under suspicion, but the bad temper of a woman she hardly knew. Bad temper was dangerous, infectious: It disturbed the carefully created peace.

"Now I'll leave you to it," the nurse said. "Remember you must indicate your choice between options, or you'll be registered as uncooperative, and we don't want that to happen, do we? If you feel the need to explain anything, just start talking - the machine will record everything you say."

Gathering her files, she went into the adjoining room. Esther waited. She knew what to expect.

There would be an apparently unexplained pause before the image portrayer came on, long enough to increase any patient's nervousness. Since scientific education was reserved only for the Keepers, most citizens were already in a state of superstitious terror of anything mechanical. They paid extra taxes because a print-out said they were in arrears, even agreed to send their children into voluntary re-education because a standard letter said they had failed a personality probe.

It was no use telling them the dream machines were just pieces of metal and microchip. The machines offered illusions of beautiful women apparently waiting their pleasure, or trips to Hawaii in their lunch hour. When they returned home their own private cablevision offered a choice of twenty dreams after dinner; when they slept, sweet music lulled them.

And like all things, they suspected, their pleasure must have a darker side, nightmares which could reduce even a hardened criminal to screaming terror. Rather than venture into such black holes of the mind they agreed to sign committals and went off quietly with their case packed the night before. Tony for instance, poor weak Tony, had signed on the dotted line and kissed the children goodbye.

To control her fear Esther investigated the machinery about her. It would obviously appeal to every sense through the power of suggestion. There would be a bewildering variety of choices offered her at great speed. In that lay the trap.

When the dreams started, they were surprisingly shabby. The console lit up, offering a range of choices: water, fire, childhood, travel, God, love.... The lights went out too quickly for her to read them all and she pressed 'Fairground'. At once the screen was filled with images of a colourful festival, lights swinging and music blaring. She was shown the various stalls, voices shouting to her to try each game. By pressing one of the knobs, she could aim a ball or throw a hoop; for some moments she played, amused at her increasing skill. Then the illusion changed, taking her on a moon roundabout with a group of laughing children. It was as if all the most pleasant memories of childhood were being created in and around her, until nothing else mattered. Abruptly the scene changed, and she was in a schoolroom being asked questions about citizenship.

At once her mind was in control again, warning of the danger. "True. False. True. True," she answered quickly, giving the answers she'd been taught.

It was a technique she came to recognise. The subject was lulled by pleasurable images which were suddenly followed by a string of rapid but vital questions. After this there came a pause during which the subject began to worry. In a society still terrified by the civil war of 2027 individualism was a threat to stability, and a wrong answer could result in the assessment of 'dissident' being given. The more intelligent one was, the more prone to doubt - and ultimately making a mistake.

Esther stared at the lamp above her, slowly repeating the word 'resist' to herself until it became a kind of mantra, blocking out all fear.

As suddenly as they had stopped, the illusions began again. This time she was given no choice of topic; images of childhood appeared in close succession. With a sense of shock, she recognised her own mother, standing holding her hand at a Keeper's Day rally. Other pictures followed: herself leading a moral education class at school, standing in jeans at a youth camp, waiting at the civil registry office in her best suit....

Esther was thoroughly frightened now, wanting to tear the bands from her arms and temple, knowing they must be registering a rise in body sweat and pulse rate, yet she controlled the impulse. The training had been sufficient. It was good to know that it could withstand a real-life test.

At last the illusions returned to their usual pattern. Esther made the necessary choices without effort. She pressed the button for peace when offered a choice between that and freedom and pressed the same button again when offered knowledge as the other alternative. Immediately she was rewarded by images of a South Sea

Island accompanied by soft music. A few more routine questions followed, then the nurse was beside her.

"There now," the nurse said, in a voice one uses to well behaved children, "That wasn't too bad, was it? You collect your little ones and have a nice cup of tea." She shuffled her papers. "If you don't hear from us, you 'll know you've been given a clean bill of health."

Fetching the children, who were quarrelsome after so long without her, Esther took the tram service to Moss Edge and her maisonette. Who had taken those films of her mother? Was she being watched all those years ago, or was it normal practice to take pictures of people? In those early years she had not been registered as a dissident. As an intellectual she would have been suspect of course, but they had thought her position as a State Welfare Officer protected her. She had behaved in a boringly normal manner, belonging to her local vigilante group, cleaning the car on Sundays, mowing the lawn.... And yet someone somewhere had been making a record of her actions, even while Esther was a toddler. Perhaps she herself was being photographed? Come to think of it, how had those pictures of her schooldays been taken?

Now that her thoughts had turned to her mother Esther felt calmer. "If we organise ourselves properly" she heard her mother's voice saying, "We can have the Keepers out in less than a decade." Her timescale had proved unrealistic, for she had underestimated the power of pleasure to satisfy and stultify. The older members had grown bitter and had resorted to terrorism, whereupon they'd been classified as mentally ill and placed in institutions for 'treatment'. But others had taken over, younger women who could resist the public dream... from within the system itself.

Instead of walking up the six flights of stairs as she usually did, that being one of the few quiet places where she could think, Esther allowed the children to persuade her to take the lift. Tiredly she opened the door on her own world. The audiovision greeted her, a babbling compere announcing some all-star prize competition. It was impossible to turn him off since the central controls were operated by the Keepers, but she could change the programme. She wanted to cry but was afraid the sound would be heard next door. Unhappiness was forbidden. Hurriedly taking a ready meal from the freezer, she put it in the microwave oven, then transferred it to the holding oven. It was six o'clock. The children must be exhausted. Still, she must dress them quickly, ready for the park. Putting Sally in her buggy and finding a ball for Tim, she set off.

By the time they arrived at the play area the other woman was sitting on the moon roundabout with her baby on her knee. Coming across casually, she put her older child into the swing next to Sally. "I was afraid you'd been picked up," she whispered.

"I was." The hinges rasped above them. "For routine trial. I think I did all right, but you've no way of knowing, have you?"

"The group meets at the relaxation centre tomorrow, eight o'clock. We have another three members - vetted and cleared. I'll leave you to contact number 125."

Lifting Sally out of the swing, Esther carried her across to the seesaw where Tim was playing. She had survived the day. Sighing, she prepared for another evening trying to ignore the audiovision machine. In such a cloying, synthetic world it was hard to know reality from illusion. The old woman sitting there so quietly in the shelter for instance - why was she there so often? She appeared harmless enough, but was that an illusion? One survived only by assuming the apparently real was a deception. They must change their meeting place, just in case. The thrill of the chase made her smile inwardly. To be hunted was at least to be fully alive; safety was a form of hibernation, a sleeping comfort. Putting on the children's coats, she turned out of the park.

A few moments later the old woman gathered her knitting. Then she too went through the gate. Perfectly innocently she followed them down Moss Edge Road.

Harald's Yard

There was definitely something moving near the gate.

A cat? In the pale light from the lamp, it was hard to tell. Her breath was settling on the window. Pulling her sleeve down, Helen cleaned a hole in the mist and stared out again. She'd never felt nervous before. As soon as the agent showed her the studio flat, she'd taken it. Though Harald's Yard was dark it was near the centre of town, down a passage off the main shopping area. Few tourists ventured through the arch and there were no neighbours to bother her, just the back doors of an empty shop unit and a restaurant, she had not yet worked out which in the beautiful jumble of roofs. She was too busy to be lonely, earning as much as she could to buy her own place. Besides, the hundreds of feet she could hear on the main street were constant company.

Leaving the gate open made her feel vulnerable, though. With workmen replacing pipes across the yard and then being held up by the archaeologists, the gate into the passageway had been unlocked for three nights now. It was a local regulation one of the men explained. In a city as old as York you had to be careful where you dug, and if you found something, you had to notify the authorities. A job could be held up for months, even years, like at Hungate. Hopefully the academics would have a quick rummage and say work could start again. Meanwhile he and his team would go elsewhere.

Frowning, Helen tried to focus on the mound near the gate. Perhaps it was one of the workmen's signs flapping? She could go out and investigate, but it was a dismal December night. The door to her building had a modern lock and bolt. She was safer staying inside. Giving herself a mental shake, Helen turned from the window and went back to bed.

In the morning her nervousness seemed silly. She was on early shift and got ready quickly. There was no sick feeling in her stomach, not like she used to feel each morning at her last job. She smiled, thinking of colleagues still shaking their heads at her stupidity: chucking a well-paid job just because she'd gone to York for a weekend and fallen in love with the city. They would think she was mad.

She would have gone mad if she'd stayed Helen reflected, or at least been sick with stress for months. Besides, why would she want to return to travelling on the underground smelling someone's armpit, when she could walk to work in less than ten minutes? True, her job at Marks and Spencer's was temporary and paid far less, but she enjoyed it. She loved the Christmas bustle, loved being able to leave her work behind instead of having to bring a briefcase home. More than anything, she liked the sense that what she was doing was real, not just playing with money to make more money and for what? So, someone at the top would be paid an obscene bonus and buy another house? How many houses did you need?

Even now Helen could feel herself getting hot and angry. "You've left it all behind," she said to herself firmly. After Christmas she would get a permanent job, one that used her degree, but she was not going back to London. If she could, she would stay in York.

A grey dawn was breaking over the rooftops as Helen locked her front door and crossed the yard. She paused at the hole near the gate. It was nearly a foot deeper. The old pipes had gone, and water was seeping into the bottom. The archaeologists had been busy yesterday, going down another layer. There were several markers where they'd found things.

As she stepped on the boards across the hole Karen suddenly felt she was being watched. Uneasily she looked round her. It was too dark to see into the corners of the yard and the mound of earth obscured her view to the right. For a moment she was afraid. "Oh stop it!" she said to herself, going out into the passageway. Rounding the corner of a tall Victorian building, she came out into Christmas lights and chatter.

It was her half day off and for the first time in a week Helen returned to the yard in daylight. To her pleasure, the academics were still there. She had visualised elderly men with beards. Instead, a young woman in jeans and a blond ponytail greeted her. "Sorry about the gang plank," she apologised as Helen walked carefully round the hole. "We won't be more than another week or so."

"Have you found anything interesting?" Helen asked.

"Lots! You live in an exciting spot."

"Do I?"

"I'll say! We've found Victorian stuff and medieval pottery below that; even a Viking shoe, and this is well outside the area we expect to find Viking remains. Mind you, these narrow lanes are on the old Viking lay-out so I suppose we shouldn't be surprised. I'm Faye, by the way."

Helen smiled. "Hello. I'm Helen Jenkins. I live in the flat over the shop." She paused, not wanting to make a fool of herself. "One of the ghost walks came down the passage the other night. The chap leading it was spinning some tale about a Viking warrior haunting my yard."

"I've never heard that one," Faye reassured her. "He probably brought his party down here by mistake and made the story up. You don't want to mind the ghost walkers. They're mostly would-be actors; studied drama here and stayed on to lead ghost walks or scare people rigid in York Dungeon."

Helen laughed. "They scared me and my mates all right. We came for a hen weekend a couple of months ago: did the Dungeon and the ghost bus." She paused wondering how her friends were, and whether they would understand her decision. "Would you and your colleague like a cup of tea?" she asked.

"That'd be great. By the way, you've got a rough sleeper," Faye added. "He disappeared as soon as we arrived."

"Should I call the police?"

"I doubt if they'd have time to come. I wouldn't bother. He wasn't doing any harm, just sheltering round the back of the mound. "

"I never know what to do when I pass them," Helen admitted. "I always feel guilty, but the papers say you shouldn't give."

"They have shelters to go to," Faye insisted. "Giving money only encourages begging."

As twilight settled back into the yard, Helen watched the gate carefully. Even so, she missed seeing the man enter. By the time she spotted him he was curled against the back of the mound, his battered trainers catching the light. His pale, thin face was framed by a baseball cap; his trousers were held up by a woman's scarf. He looked about fifty but could have been much younger, worn out by drink and years of sleeping rough. His right hand clutched the inevitable bottle. Urgently Helen wondered what to do, but he seemed to be asleep, and she felt sorry for him. She didn't fancy passing him, but so long as he left before she went to work, she could put up with him staying.

The following morning Helen shone her torch across the yard before she set off. To her relief the man had gone. A stale smell clung around the area. Going back into the kitchen she filled a bowl of water and threw it over the soil.

For four more nights the man took up his pitch against the mound, sometimes holding a cardboard cup of coffee someone had given him, sometimes a bottle. In the run-up to Christmas Helen was working long hours and unable to meet anyone but her colleagues. It was good to see another human being, even if he was a rough sleeper. Now that the excitement of giving up her job and moving to York was fading, she was beginning to feel lonely. She began thinking of the stranger as 'Fred' and looking for him each night. All the same, on the Thursday when M and S closed late, she asked one of her male colleagues to walk back with her.

It was well after nine. A dank grey mist had descended, chilling the bones, and the lamp in the passageway scarcely reached the yard. It was impossible to see if the man was back or not. Her colleague advised getting him moved on, but Helen replied that he'd probably left, and wasn't any trouble in any case. Still, she was grateful to be seen right to her door.

As she was getting ready for bed, the mist lifted a little. Staring out of her window, Helen saw the rough sleeper was back in his usual place, though wrapped so tightly in a blanket she couldn't see his face. She hated to think of him crouched against the mound, cold and hungry.

When she left for work the following morning Helen placed a chocolate bar on the mound. By evening it had gone.

All that weekend and the following week, the hole

remained beside the gate, getting deeper and wider. It would be recorded and photographed on Friday, Faye said, then backfilled the following Monday. After that, the workmen would return, lay their pipes and make good, though with Christmas almost on them that might be in the New Year. For some reason Helen felt reluctant to tell Faye that the rough sleeper was still around, or that she felt so sorry for him she regularly left food and cups of tea for him. Put into words, it sounded a silly thing to do.

At last, the Monday arrived, and the mound of soil was loosely packed back in the hole, ready for the workmen to return. Helen wished the archaeologists goodbye, catching them just as they were leaving. She gave a sigh of relief as she prepared to lock the gate to the passageway. Then she paused, sensing a movement. The man was still in the yard, she was certain, though she couldn't see him. "I'm locking the gate in half an hour, Fred," she called. "Go, or you'll get shut in."

There was a grunt of thanks from the far corner. Then Helen went into her flat, bolting the door behind her.

All that evening Helen watched from her window, hoping to see the man leave. There was no sign of movement. The mist had settled again, a fine drizzle soaking the yard. Eating her meal as she stood there, she couldn't decide what to do. Should she lock the gate, and risk shutting Fred in? If he thought she was imprisoning him he might be awkward, angry perhaps. Should she call the police? And tell them someone might be in the yard, or might have gone? She would sound a fool.

Finally, she left the gate unlocked another night.

The following day Helen didn't have to be at work until 11.00 am. She decided to have a good look round the yard in daylight, having first checked from her window it was empty. She looked carefully around the filled hole and where the mound of soil had been. There was nothing, no fag ends or cartons, no empty bottles, nothing to suggest a man had sheltered there. Even the smell had gone. Puzzled, Karen crossed to the corner where she'd heard the man speak, but there was no sign of him there either.

Something on the soil glinted in the winter sunlight. Intrigued, Helen picked it up.

The object was small and hard, crusted in dirt. She took it back to her kitchen and gently cleaned it. A shape gradually appeared, like a little hammer. "A brooch?" she thought, feeling for a pin at the back. It must be a modern trinket she decided, dropped by someone putting rubbish in the bins. But when she dabbed the metal dry with a sheet of kitchen towel she paused in surprise. It looked like silver, though darkened with age.

"Oh Lor!" she said as she cleaned the back more carefully. "It is silver!"

She was holding a very old brooch, in the shape of a hammer. "How did the archaeologists miss this?" she wondered. It must have been swept aside when they cleared the soil. What should she do with it? It looked very old. Viking perhaps...

She would have to take it to the museum as soon

as possible.

There was just time before work. Quickly Helen wrapped the brooch in a tissue and put it in her handbag. Then she went into the yard. For a second, she paused beside the remains of the mound. "Thank you, Fred, or is it Harald?" she said aloud. "But I can't possibly keep it."

Feeling suddenly foolish, she unlocked the gate.

Jardinière

It was one of those "eureka" moments. When things start to make sense.

PC Webb would always remember that moment. He'd been getting himself a coffee down at the station (if that's what you call the brown liquid that comes out of the machine).

"Doing anything interesting Geoff?" WPC Lloyd asked. She always had time for the new recruits and Geoff Webb seemed more competent than most.

"Been getting my ear bent by a woman on Stratton Road. Reported a small tree being stolen from her garden. I could understand if it had been in a pot, but she was adamant it was dug up. I can't see a gang of ruthless gardeners wandering round, carrying spades."

WPC Lloyd frowned. "Doug also had a complaint about a tree disappearing. I think it was a conifer. I've got a message about bushes too."

"That's a coincidence." Even as PC Webb spoke, he knew it probably wasn't. Stealing plants didn't rank high on the crime-scale, but it was a bit different. "Do you mind if I see your message?" he asked. "I can look into it."

"Help yourself," Jane replied. She poured the rest of her tea away in disgust.

In total, Geoff found sixteen reports of missing plants. Most were small trees, but some were flowering bushes. His knowledge of gardening wasn't great, but he found an ally in Sgt Barlow who had green enough fingers for them both.

"What's a fuchsia?" Geoff asked.

"It's a small bush, with red flowers. The flowers droop down. Was it in a tub or planted outside?"

Geoff rustled through the papers on his desk. "In a pot; terracotta and shaped like a Grecian urn."

"Very nice, I'm sure. So that makes eleven missing tubs or pots and seven trees. That's quite a nice haul. If this goes on, the thieves will be able to set up their own stately home."

"I'll pay the local garden centre a visit," Geoff suggested. "Would you join me? I can identify a pot like a Grecian urn, but I won't have a clue whether it's got a fuchsia in it."

"If they've got any sense, they'll have taken the plants out of their pots and put them in something else," Sgt Barlow suggested.

"How will we know whether we've found someone's fuchsia, or a similar one that was already for sale?" Geoff asked.

"We won't, unless someone's marked their pots with infra-red. The thieves will have smashed any with names on."

A search of the local garden centre proved pointless. There were plenty of fuchsias and lots of terracotta pots, including several like Grecian urns. None of the pots looked used, however.

Geoff drove home at the end of his shift, disgruntled. He had his first unusual crime and there seemed no way he could crack it. Not only did all plants look alike to him, but how could anyone identify which terracotta pot was which? He was beginning to think it was the perfect crime, as long as you didn't get caught digging someone's garden up.

That must mean the thieves struck at night. Surely no one would steal trees or bushes in daylight? And how would they carry them? Geoff didn't know how heavy a small conifer would be, but he couldn't imagine thieves walking down the street with one under their arm.

He almost missed the traffic lights turning red. As he waited, he glanced out of his window towards the pub car park. A sign caught his attention. "Fantastic plants" it read.

Signalling, Geoff pulled in. The selection was small. Sgt Barlow would have been most unimpressed. There was only a dozen or so terracotta pots and a few small trees, one of which looked like a Christmas tree. Was that a conifer, Geoff wondered? He also found a small bush with red flowers cascading over the side of a black plastic pot. Perhaps this was a fuchsia?

He knew not to get excited. Even if one of the neighbours swore blind that it was their tree or pot, it would never amount to a proper identification.

He watched the two salesmen. One was a young lad, probably no more than 14. Hopefully he was just doing a Saturday job and had nothing to do with the thefts. The other guy was more interesting. In his early 30s, he looked like he hadn't shaved for a couple of days. The bottoms of his jeans were frayed and the knees sagged. Geoff could imagine this guy sneaking through someone's garden with a spade.

Deciding to test a theory he went up to the sales counter, a rickety trestle table. "Hi," he said to the young boy. "I'd like to buy something for my mother. She doesn't like cut flowers as they die too quickly. I was wondering if you'd got a fuchsia."

The lad shrugged and turned to Mr Dishevelled. "Do we have any fooshchas?" he asked.

"How should I know? If he wants gardening advice, tell him to go to the garden centre. She don't pay me enough to mug up on gardening."

Geoff smiled as he told the boy not to worry. So, the guy with the saggy jeans might be hired muscle, but he didn't have the knowledge to choose what to steal.

A petite blond lady appeared. She was in her 60s, but well preserved. "Did I hear you asking about fuchsias, young man?" she asked. Her teeth were perfect and dazzling white.

"I'd like to buy one for my mother."

"Well, here's a lovely one," the woman replied. "A hardy variety so she can leave it outside all year. It'll die back over the next few months and it's best to prune it just before spring. But the flowers are ever so pretty and it's just £5. It'd be double that at the garden centre."

Geoff felt in his pocket for a fiver. Perhaps he could claim it back. "How can you sell such lovely plants at such a good price?" he asked.

He could feel the older salesman staring at him. "Oh," the lady smiled, "I grow these in my little allotment. Jacob and Paul here help me out selling them at weekends."

Geoff nodded, paid and left. He wasn't convinced. The lady obviously knew her stuff, but he couldn't see her digging an allotment. He didn't think she'd done a day's hard labour in her life.

Inevitably, the fuchsia identification was inconclusive. It was the same type as one stolen from Stratton Street, but the owner thought it was bigger. Unless it had stretched now it was out of its Grecian urn. Geoff knew that if he bought the little Christmas tree, he'd have no more luck matching that. There was no way he would persuade his Inspector to raid a plant stall.

A few days later WPC Lloyd called him across. "There's been another theft," she said. "Here's the address. Pot plants this time."

"I doubt I'll be able to do much," Geoff replied. But he looked at the address and headed over there.

Mr Broome was in his sixties, a precise and neat man. He looked like he'd been something senior before he'd retired. His plump wife had clearly been a beauty in her youth. Even now her clear blue eyes seemed to bore into Geoff as he stood on their doorstep. They insisted on seeing his identification before letting him in.

"You can't be too careful these days," Mrs Broome said, showing Geoff into a large sitting room. He sank into an armchair, wondering whether he'd need a hand to get back out. "What can you tell me about the theft of your pots?" he began.

"I've made a list of the missing items," Mr Broome replied. Geoff wouldn't have been surprised to find they'd got an inventory of all their belongings. He took the list, just as Mrs Broome reappeared with a dainty pink tea service on a tray.

"This is very useful," Geoff nodded. "The only problem will be proving the pots belong to you, even if we do find them." He felt he ought to be honest.

"The security marking should help." Mrs Broome poured the tea with a smug smile.

"Excellent," Geoff said. "What form does the marking take?"

"We have one of those special security pens," Mr Broome replied. "We've written our postcode on all our movables. You can't see it with the naked eye., only a florescent light."

He moved towards the bureau and reappeared with an innocuous looking pen and an oblong light. Turning the light on, he shone it across the coffee table. A postcode appeared on one of its legs.

"This is fantastic!" Geoff exclaimed. "I have a lead as to who the thieves might be, so if you'll allow me to borrow your light I can check if they have your pots."

"Before you charge off, PC Webb," Mr Broome replied, "you may also wish to speak to our daughter.

She saw the thieves in the act, last night."

Geoff couldn't believe his ears. Things were getting better and better. If the daughter could also supply a description of the thieves, he should be home and dry.

"This is Elizabeth, PC Webb," Mrs Broome was making the introductions. Geoff smiled encouragingly.

"Tell the policeman what you told us this morning, dear." Mr Broome put a hand on her shoulder.

"It was late last night," she spoke simply. "It was dark. I heard a noise. I looked and saw a man with one of our pots. He took it to a van. He came back and took another one. Then another one and one more."

"That's right," Mrs Broome interrupted. "A total of four pots are missing, as you'll see from the list. Fortunately, I moved my Acer to the conservatory on Sunday, so the thieves didn't get that."

Geoff smiled. "Did you see what the man looked like?" he asked.

"He was scruffy," Elizabeth replied. "His jeans were really dirty." Geoff swore he heard Mrs Broome tut at the thought of someone dirty near her house.

It sounded like the older man at the plant sale. "Did you see his face?" Geoff continued.

"No. He had a van, white with some words on the side. I think it said Paul something."

Geoff's mind was working. Paul was one of the names the woman used. "Did you see anyone with him?" he asked.

"Yes, but she didn't get out."

"She: are you sure it was a woman?" Geoff was writing furiously in his notebook.

"She was small and blond." Elizabeth turned to her mother. "But I think it was pretend blond."

"She probably dyes her hair." Mrs Broome sniffed in disapproval.

"This is extremely useful," Geoff was closing his notebook.

"That's not all," Mrs Broome stopped him. "Elizabeth followed them. She knows where they went."

"She followed them?" Geoff was incredulous. This was the middle of the night; they were in a van, and she was on foot in her pyjamas. How could she possibly have followed them?

"I feel I should explain." It was Mr Broome talking now. "Our daughter has an unusual talent. When she's asleep, she has moments when her soul leaves her body. That's how she was able to see the thefts, even though her bedroom is actually at the back. If she says she followed the thieves, she means that her soul did. I can assure you that her body never left her bedroom. We always lock her door."

Geoff was feeling a little light-headed. The description he'd just written down was from an out of body experience. How could he possibly use it? He'd be a laughing stock at the 'station. He didn't know what to say. His instinct was to stand up and run out or look round the room for hidden cameras. Perhaps this was some weird reality TV show or a joke. Without any real thought, he turned to Elizabeth. "Can you describe where the van went, please?"

Mr and Mrs Broome nodded approvingly at his question.

Elizabeth smiled. "Of course. They drove down the road and turned left into Lee Lane. Then they went right into Duncan Road and down a little track after the red house. Then they went to a garage with a dirty blue door. There were loads of pots in there."

It was force of habit, rather than any actual belief on Geoff's part, that had made him write her description down. He made his excuses and got up, assuring the Broomes that he'd leave no stone unturned in looking for their pots.

"Hadn't you better go straight to the garages and see if the pots are still there?" Mr Broome asked.

Aware that the whole family were watching him, PC Webb felt obliged to walk down the road, taking the route the van was supposed to have travelled.

To his surprise he found the little track. There was only one red house, numbered 15, and the track lay between it and number 17. A sign indicated Garages for houses 11-21. He calculated there would be six garages (unless the neighbourhood was too superstitious to have a number 13). With growing surprise, he saw that the third garage along did indeed have a blue door. He couldn't just open the door without consent or a warrant, so he decided to call the 'station. He didn't need to say why he wanted to know who lived at 15 Duncan Road.

Once Sgt Barlow had spotted that the owner was the mother of a known criminal, Paul Norton, the rest happened with surreal speed. A judge issued a warrant to search the garage, on the basis of Geoff's identification of Paul Norton as the plant salesman with zero knowledge of plants. Not much searching was required; the only thing in the garage, other than the pots, plants, bushes and trees, was Paul's van. Inside the van, they found the pots belonging to Mr and Mrs Broome. Each had been marked with the invisible postcode. It was enough for an arrest.

The only potential fly in the ointment was Elizabeth. Geoff hadn't told anyone about his conversation with her. He couldn't tell people about her so-called out of body experience, without fearing it would jeopardise the conviction. But he also couldn't tear pages out of his notebook. Any defence would demand to know what those pages contained.

Fortunately, although Paul would never have owned up, his mother confessed. Her old age pension wasn't keeping her in the manner to which she was accustomed. It seemed the thefts were her idea, having noticed how many of her neighbours were proud gardeners, and how busy the local garden centre was. Jacob, the young lad, was cleared although he now needed a new Saturday job. Geoff became famous within the 'station for clearing up a large number of unsolved thefts within his rookie year. He didn't let it go to his head.

Almost a month later, Geoff was sorting through his phone messages, when he saw a name that he recognised. Mr Broome had called and wanted to see him urgently. Not trusting any conversation with the Broomes to the telephone, Geoff went to see him.

"It's Elizabeth," Mr Broome explained. He was clearly worried. Geoff wondered if she'd tried to make a bid for freedom, but he was wrong.

Elizabeth entered the room. "I had a dream," she said. Geoff raised an eyebrow at Mr Broome.

"She means she had another episode when her soul roamed around on its own," Mr Broome explained, as if it was the most natural event in the world.

"And what did you see?" Geoff asked.

"I saw a man kill a woman."

Etcetera

———

The cafe was busy. For a second Alice panicked. There was no room by the window. Fortunately, a couple left and the young waitress led her to their table. "Let me clear up for you," the girl said as Alice nearly knocked a cup over.

"Calm down!" Alice said to herself. "If you go on as you are, you'll make a mess of things."

She looked out onto King's Square. The busker was working the crowd, asking them to cheer a little girl as she ran to a kitchen plunger he had placed on the flagstones. Alice had seen his act several times. "How to turn two minutes' preparation into a ten-minute show," she thought, smiling. Then she reached in her bag and took out the folded paper. Trying not to let her neighbours see, she read it for the tenth time. It sounded well enough.

"ATTRACTIVE, intelligent, lady, late 30's; g.s.h. Enjoys walking, travelling, dancing etc. Easy, relaxed person. Widowed. Would like to meet caring male for friendship and outings."

Alice was still not sure about the 'etc'. Did it imply things she didn't intend? Knocking six years off her age was probably a mistake too. Truth usually came out, but would any man want to meet a woman already turned forty? Once they got to know her and found that she was young in mind, her age wouldn't matter.

Anxiously she looked at people near her. No one fitted the description Bob had given. Unobtrusively, she studied the photograph he had sent her. Perhaps there wasn't a seat near the window when he arrived. Turning round, she looked further into the café. No, there was no one anywhere who could be the youthful looking sportsman lounging in his tennis kit. The man sitting at the other table in the window bore some resemblance, but not a lot. He was older and balder. Nor was he 'athletic'.

Besides, she knew him vaguely. He lived in one of the mews flats opposite. They had spoken briefly when she pipped him to the last parking space on the road. He had seemed a good sort, making a joke of it rather than getting cross. He certainly didn't seem the sort to advertise on Lonely.com.

Once again, Alice unfolded the other advert. It had appeared the same day as her own, in the section, Men Seeking Women. "Divorced, 5'9", 35, caring, honest, g s of h, into sports, cinema, music, eating out etc., seeks female 30's-40's for fun, friendship and hopefully romance."

Her stomach lurched as she reread the description. It was so odd the way they had both advertised the same day, and then e-mailed each other. So very odd. As Bob wrote, it seemed like Fate. Alice had been sure that for once she had struck lucky. And now he hadn't turned up.

"He isn't here, Love," she said to herself, and realised she was speaking to Jim again. She couldn't get out of the habit of mentally talking to her dead husband! Sighing she looked out of the window again. The crowd in the square surged forward. The busker was coming to the serious part of his act, getting out the chains and relighting the burning stick. That was a good thing about living in York - there was always something going on. If you were lonely, all you had to do was go into town and watch the tourists, or enjoy a bit of free entertainment – well, almost free. It could make you feel worse though, she reflected: all those happy families and friends enjoying a day out together…

Giving herself a shake mentally she watched the crowd in front of her. The busker was almost hidden now, just his head and shoulders showing above his audience as he balanced on his ladder.

Her order had arrived, and Alice smiled her thanks. Inwardly she wished she was in her usual spot on the riverbank, watching the geese and the boats while she ate her sandwich. Her throat was going tight with disappointment, but there was no point in getting emotional. Firmly she put the photo and the printouts into the envelope. Then she looked at the clock. It was ten past one. She had only been five minutes late reaching the cafe. Surely Bob could have waited five minutes?

...

"Divorced, 5'9", 35, caring, honest, g s of h," sat beside the window and stared into his coffee. He felt a fool. What on earth had possessed him to come? To advertise in the first place? Loneliness, he supposed. Like all the other poor lonely blokes who tried Lonely.com. He had had enough of going back to his flat on his own, to eat a freezer meal in front of the TV. Working such long hours, it was difficult to meet people and impossible to meet decent women of his own age. They were all married, or the sort you were wise to avoid.

Besides, he wasn't any good at speaking to women. He could always feel how bald he was going on top, and the way his stomach was beginning to bulge over his belt. He used to look better, but that was when he had Beth to cook for him, and time for a social life. A sportsman always looks bad when he goes to seed. He ought to have sent an up-to-date photograph, but he hadn't had the nerve. It was daft taking five years off his age too. Still, there was no sense in putting a woman off before he started.

Sighing, he took out the photograph Amanda had sent him. She didn't look much like an Amanda. It probably wasn't her real name. Even he had used his second name when he replied. You had to be careful. Everyone warned that a date with someone you'd met on-line was risky.

Once again, Bob looked around the room. There was no one who matched the photograph. All the women were older and more, well, worn out he supposed. The woman in the photo was genuinely beautiful, not brassy and dressed to kill like the hen party passing across the square. Funnily enough, she reminded him of the woman at the table near him. She had the same dark eyes.

Now that was odd. He knew her slightly. She lived in one of the flats on the other side of the courtyard. She'd had a cheek, nicking his parking spot just as he was backing into it, but he'd been in a good mood after a weekend with his son and hadn't had the heart to be angry. He wondered what she was doing in Chloe's café. Presumably she worked in town as well. It was probably her lunch hour.

Reflectively he drank his coffee. It was nearly quarter past one. Amanda wasn't going to turn up. She had lost her nerve perhaps, as he had nearly lost his. Or maybe she had already found someone - some man who had replied quicker than he had and was just what she was looking for. Well, there wasn't much point in waiting around. He might as well go back to work.

In some ways Bob was quite relieved. It was easier not to have to start getting to know someone, and let himself in for goodness knows what? One break-up was enough. It always looked so easy on the films, but in real life it wasn't. Deep inside him, he still hurt. He still missed Beth too, however much he pretended he didn't.

…

They reached the door at the same time, almost pushing

into each other. "After you," Alice said, flushing.

"No, after you."

Still red with embarrassment, Alice held the door open so that he could follow her.

"I know you, don't I?" Bob asked.

"I live in the flats opposite you," Alice replied. She hoped he had forgotten the parking episode.

A great cheer went up from the crowd. "He managed to escape," Bob remarked drily.

"He usually does," Alice agreed smiling.

He couldn't help but notice she was near to tears, her mouth quivering slightly. "You look as though you've been stood up," he said in sympathy.

"I have," Alice admitted. "My date obviously thought better of it. I must get back to work."

"Same here."

As they both seemed to be going the same way, they crossed the square together, avoiding the crowd round the busker. The entrance to the Shambles was packed, a party of Japanese tourists trying to leave, just as a college party was trying to enter.

"It's busy today," Bob remarked. "Oh, of course. The schools have broken up. Where are you heading?"

"The library."

"I'm going to the station. Four elbows are better than two. Shall we walk down together?"

Smiling, Alice nodded. "Are you a train driver?" she asked

"No such luck. I book rail tickets and sort out people's journeys. I used to dream of driving a steam engine.

This is the closest I can get paid for. I volunteer on the North York Moors Railway on my holidays. That's when I come alive." He laughed in embarrassment. "I'm a fully-fledged Railway geek."

"Me too, only my engines are smaller."

He looked at her in surprise. Her eyes really were rather beautiful; dark and expressive. "Model railways," she explained. "I'm a member of the York Model Engineers group. I used to long to be an engineer when I was a girl, but people laughed at me, so I went into library work. I enjoy it, but like you say, I come alive at weekends."

They had reached St Sampson's Square. A young girl was singing a number from 'Phantom', her voice soaring above the babble. For a second, they paused to listen. "She can sing," Alice remarked. Quickly she crossed and dropped a coin in the girl's dish. "I always like to give if they've genuinely got talent," she explained afterwards.

"I usually do, but I've got no change," Bob said apologetically as they crossed the square. A boy was bouncing up and down on the bungy jump near them, squealing as he went higher and higher.

"I went on one of those things once," Bob added "Only it was twice the height. It was a week before I worked out which way was up."

Alice laughed. "Where was that?"

"New Zealand. I lived there for a while."

With interest, Alice turned to him. "That sounds interesting," she remarked, glancing at his face. It was odd. He did look a bit like the man in the photograph, around the nose and mouth in particular. "We have an Open Day next Sunday," she added. "Why don't you pop in and have a look at our engines? There'll be a bit of an exhibition too." Then she flushed, realising he might misunderstand. "I might be there myself, I'm not sure yet."

"Thanks. I might look in. Presumably I can get details on-line?"

The smell of hot dogs reminded Alice she'd only eaten half her cheese scone. She had been too upset to eat more. If she didn't buy something more now, she would be starving all afternoon. "I'll have to pop into a shop for something," she said.

The more she looked at him, the more certain Alice was that he was the man who'd replied to her advert. It would be unkind to say so, though. He was obviously horribly embarrassed by the whole situation. She would let him think she hadn't realised. "Of course," she added. "Or I can drop some leaflets through your door."

As she spoke Alice remembered she didn't know his real name. She would have to ask around.

"I'd better get a move on," Bob said glancing at his watch and then at her face. It was definitely the face in the photograph, but that portrait must have been taken when she was younger or perhaps before grief added the lines around her eyes and flecked her hair with grey. He wouldn't say anything, however. She was obviously terribly embarrassed. He would let her think he hadn't realised. Still, it was good to know someone else could make a fool of themselves...

"I don't know your name," he called, but by then she had gone.

Apple Blossom

Maria shivered, turning towards Simon. "What was that?" she whispered. "The ghost?" Until then she hadn't believed the legend.

"Ghosts don't scatter stones," Simon replied. "Look!" He pointed to where a fine rain of gravel fell behind the house. "Someone slipped. But what are they doing on the hill in the dark? We'd better see if Miss B's ok."

After three rings of the bell an eye appeared at the spy hole. "It's Simon and Maria – your new neighbours," Simon called. "There's someone prowling around. Are you alright?"

The door opened and Miss Blavaski greeted them. "Come in Darlings," she invited. "I'm fine. I was going to call. I have a present for you."

Mystified, they followed the woman down a panelled hallway and into a large lounge dominated by a grand piano. There was a strong scent, like apple blossom. Maria saw Simon frown but he said nothing. "Forgive the mess," Miss Blavaski said. "I'm working." She saw their bewilderment. "I'm a composer. That's how I earn my living, though mostly from writing practice pieces for children. This is theme music for a film but it's being stubborn. Greta isn't helping tonight."

Maria looked at the cat curled on a pile of paper. "I thought he was called Henry," she said.

Miss B laughed, crossing to fetch a carrier bag from the table. "Just a little thank you for feeding him," she explained and passed the bag to Maria. "Henry hinders rather than helps, sitting on my music. Greta's long dead of course but I like to think she keeps me company. I imagine you've heard the story at the Fox and Grapes?"

Uncertainly Simon nodded. "An ancestor perhaps?" he asked tactfully.

"My Great Grandmother. Slipped from the rocks while she was waiting for her lover. Great Grand Daddy may have given her a push. "

"So, she really existed?" Maria asked.

"Oh yes. I have photos. She was lovely, and a very clever musician. She toured the music halls as Greta Blavaski before she married. I took her surname when I went professional – much more interesting than Angela Brown. I'm not surprised she had a lover. She must have been bored to tears here." The woman smiled and glanced at the clock. "You must come for drinks sometime, but I have a deadline to meet this week."

Taking the hint Simon and Maria left, thanking her for the gift.

"I want to see if anyone's still on the hill," Simon insisted afterwards. "Come on. We've both got torches and there's a good moon."

They walked carefully up the track as far as the beacon stone.

There was no one about. In relief they stood in the moonlight looking at the house below. "Can you smell apple blossom?" Maria asked in surprise. "It must have got stuck in my nostrils."

"Yes," Simon said. He shook his head in bewilderment. "There's a bit of the legend I didn't tell you. I thought it was trivial. People say that whenever the ghost appears you can smell the perfume she wore: Apple Blossom."

Sophie's Choice

———

He slipped. Cursing, he shot out a hand to steady himself, his fingers colliding with wet tree. A sharp pain oozed up his arm from the impact. He paused, teetering on the muddy bank, but didn't fall.

He realised he'd been holding his breath. Slowly he exhaled. Shifting the bag again, he stood up straight. It was only a few more paces to the water. He knew he could make it. He had to make it.

The handle was cutting into his hand. It was made to hold full diving kit, but the wheeled bag wasn't designed for this weight. Her weight: her dead weight. He still couldn't believe how long it had taken to get her body into her swimsuit. Stuffing it into a carrier, large enough to take a week's scuba equipment, had been easy in comparison.

Despite the pain in his hand, he smiled at how well everything had gone. He'd managed to fetch his dive bag from the attic without Sophie even commenting. She was used to him going off on diving weekends. When they first met, she would have come with him, but she had other interests now…

Dawn was still at least an hour away. The moon rippled on the lake's surface, glinting on liquid black. A splash to his right made him jump. Staring, he spotted a small duck, startled by his presence. He relaxed. No one would worry about wild fowl noises, not around here.

The mud was sticky this close to the water's edge. He'd kept to the stony path till now. After so little rain it wouldn't retain wheel prints. Here, though every mark would show. He would have to carry the bag the last two yards and remove any tell-tale footprints afterwards. It was a good job there was a lot of dead branches around after the last flood. He could use one to scrape the mud back.

Then he had a thought. What about her feet? It had to look like she'd walked to the lake for her morning swim.

He'd been so careful planting that idea in her head. What a great way to exercise, he'd said. Why pay to join a gym when they lived right next to a lake? He knew she loved swimming; knew she'd latch on to the thought of getting fit whilst saving money. That was one thing he couldn't fault her on. She was never extravagant.

She'd need to leave tracks, he realised. Gingerly laying the dive bag down, he unzipped it slowly from one end, finding painted toenails. He was pleased he'd guessed right; he didn't particularly want to look at her face again. He pulled her feet, so they stuck out at a crazy angle. Straddling the bag, and tipping it forward, he 'walked' her towards the water. A holdall with legs, he smiled to himself.

He was glad she was so small. 'Dainty' he used to call her. It'd been easy to grab her heels and pull them up, so her head went under the bath water. He hadn't needed to hold her down. He'd been surprised how quickly she'd gulped enough water to drown. There'd be no sign of a struggle when they found her body.

He'd even made sure there was no bubble-bath in the water in case they analysed her lungs. She'd been a bit surprised by the lack of foam and by the greenness of the water, but he'd been ahead of her yet again. It was a special sea salt treatment, he'd explained, good for her skin. She wasn't to know that he'd been hoarding lake water for three days to fill the tub. He'd even heated it up for her. At least her last bath was a warm one. He wasn't that cruel.

Finally reaching the lake, he opened the bag fully. Pushing forwards, he tipped its contents into the water. Then he 'launched' his late wife with a gentle shove to the sole of her foot. He watched as Sophie floated away, face down.

Lifting the now empty diving bag upright, he found a branch and brushed it around the mud to remove any sign of his presence. Humming softly, he returned up the path, to the road between the silent houses. He knew he had to dispose of the evidence. He'd seen enough TV forensics: the dive bag would be full of her DNA. But he had that sorted. too. Cutting the plastic with the Stanley knife he'd brought, he squashed the bag back to its frame, and dumped it in a neighbour's wheelie bin. The bin men would arrive in the next few hours.

Beautiful timing on his part: picking bin day for her last 'swim' and working back. It hadn't been hard making sure she was in late the night before, tired out, so he could offer to run her bath. All he had to do was arrange an evening conference call and she did the rest. He knew she'd jump at the chance of a night out, 'with the girls' she'd said. He didn't need to ask who her companion had really been. He knew already and it wasn't female.

He'd leave for the office shortly, to go to the breakfast meeting he'd arranged weeks ago: the perfect alibi. It would be hours before anyone noticed Sophie was missing. With any luck, one of the stuck-up neighbours might even spot her bloated body. That would wipe the smug look off their faces. The thought amused him.

He'd act the distraught husband later. Demand to know how his wife, such a strong swimmer, could possibly drown in the lake. Be horrified at the suggestion she might have killed herself on purpose, that there were any problems in their marriage. After all, no one knew about Sophie's lover. Even he, or rather especially he, wasn't meant to know.

Ironic, he mused: Sophie thinking she'd got one over him. She was so sure he hadn't a clue. She wasn't to know he'd been tracking her movements for weeks. Ever since that night she'd left her phone in the lounge, and he'd seen the text: "See you tomorrow, love Mark xxx".

Working out which Mark had taken a few days.

After that, it had been easy following them to restaurants and seedy hotels. The whole time she'd been wrapped in her illicit love, he'd been plotting his revenge.

It was her choice: her fault. No one cheated on him. He'd warned her last time. He thought he'd made it quite clear what would happen if she crossed him again. Clearly, she hadn't believed him, even with a black eye as a reminder. That was unfortunate. They'd lie to the neighbours: pretend she'd tripped on the back steps. She was so clumsy no one questioned them. This time he'd made sure there was nothing to see.

He was approaching the cottage. Closing the door gently he stood in the kitchen, too keyed up to go back to sleep. He fancied a cup of coffee. As he waited for the kettle to boil, he started to smile. That would teach her to cheat on him. No woman did that to him and got away with it.

He flicked the radio on as the coffee brewed. Suddenly he stopped short and listened closely. "Strike over pensions hits refuse collection," the voice intoned. The bins wouldn't be emptied for a week at least. He suddenly felt cold to his stomach. So that's what Sophie had been prattling on about last night. He'd been so focussed on his plans; he hadn't listened to her.

Would the dive bag be discovered? Should he go back to retrieve it? Suddenly, for the first time, he didn't know what to do. He felt the rage building inside him. How dare Sophie choose to die on the day of the bin strike? How could she do that to him?

Safe House

Cars sped past. "What better place for a safe house?" the policewoman had asked. No passers-by or curtain twitchers, just an old cottage marooned by traffic.

Now the waiting was ending. Tomorrow she would be in Court. And when the trial was over her new life would begin. Janette Johnson would be no more, replaced by Ruthie Desmond, with passport and flight and a Melbourne address. Janette would be remembered only as the mousey girl in Accounts who was brave – or foolish - enough to cause one of the biggest fraud investigations in a decade. Not even a mysterious fire at her flat could dissuade her. 'Brave little accountant' the papers had called her.

She didn't feel very brave now. Sighing, she went downstairs to make yet another cup of tea. She would have liked to go into the back garden but even between its hedges she wouldn't be safe. A drone could spot her from above. So she prowled about the house while the kettle boiled, re-examining the treasures she had found: a pencil on the sideboard, a shampoo sachet in the bathroom, a hairpin on the dresser. To her delight she found another, a sliver of mirror behind the clock. It must have been wiped clean of DNA then deliberately left. The Leavings, as she called them, had probably started accidentally when a cleaner failed to clean, then been picked up as a comforting idea. What could she leave that would say something about herself?

Suddenly the front doorbell rang. In terror she froze. "Pizza!" a male voice called. "Pizza delivery!"

Hardly daring to breathe she remained silent.

"Pepperoni pizza for one," the voice called again.

For an instant Janette was tempted. She was sick of the microwave meals left for her. Then she told herself not to be foolish. "Whatever you do, don't open the door," her Minder had warned. "Not till you get my code on your mobile and know it's me."

The doorbell rang again, louder. Still Janette waited silently. Finally she heard footsteps leaving the porch and a motorbike revving. For another five minutes she listened, then crept to the window and peeped between the blinds. There was nothing but traffic. Shaky with fear, she sat on the sofa. Had the man made a genuine mistake or did the Syndicate know she was there? Shivering, she took refuge in sleep.

Dusk was settling in the room when she was woken by her phone buzzing. Urgently Janette grabbed it and saw the call sign. Then she waited as the Minder let herself in. "How have you been?" the woman asked.

At once the words came spilling out - how the doorbell had rung and rung - how she had hidden in the shadows hardly daring to breathe…

"Hmm," the policewoman said coolly. "Could be a genuine mistake or a bit of a problem. Not to worry. You're leaving tonight. Tomorrow you give your evidence. Then you'll be on your way."

"Where?" Janette asked.

"To your new life. How do you do - Ruthie?"

The Bread Man

"Look, there he is!"

Matt nudged Sarah with his foot. She sighed and glared at him over the top of her book. They were sitting beneath one of the large sweet-chestnut trees, shaded but still warm in the dappled sunlight.

"Who?" she asked testily.

"That guy I've told you about. The 'Bread Man'."

Sarah looked where Matt was pointing, past the ice cream kiosk.

"I can see an old guy walking by the pond, but what's wrong with that?" she asked. She wanted to go back to her book.

"Look more closely," Matt insisted. "He's so weird. He gives me the creeps the way he wanders around. He always has his bag of bread. Maybe he's trying to lure children into his house!"

"Oh, don't talk such rubbish," Sarah retorted. "He's just an old guy bringing bread for the ducks."

"Except there aren't any ducks," Matt pointed out.

This was true, Sarah thought. She looked more

closely at the man. It was hard to determine if he was young or old, or what race he was. He walked slowly, a little bent at the shoulders, but his face bore no wrinkles. His clothing, Sarah had to admit, was indeed odd. It was a beautiful August Saturday, the sky a cobalt blue with just a few wispy clouds. Sarah was in her summer dress, with a cardigan in her bag in case it got cool before they went home. Matt was in shorts and t-shirt.

The 'Bread Man' was wearing long grey trousers, brown suede loafer shoes and a red sweater. Over the top he'd added a brown sleeveless vest that looked to Sarah like it might be lined with fleece. Finally, he was wearing a furry hat, with ear flaps pulled down, and glasses. He was carrying a stick in one hand and in the other, a carrier bag. There was a hole in one corner of the bag. He was leaving a trail of white blobs of bread on the path behind him.

"I wonder what he's got the bread for," Sarah mused. "Do squirrels eat bread?"

"I've told you; he wants little kids to follow him!" Matt insisted.

"That's so ridiculous it doesn't deserve a reply," Sarah retorted. "Besides, you'd need sweets or beefburgers not bread. He's far more likely to find a flock of pigeons following him home."

"Maybe he eats pigeons for tea?" Matt grinned and ducked as Sarah took a swipe at him with her book. Baiting Sarah was his favourite pastime, even if it was too easy at times.

They started home around seven. At first, they didn't

see the little line of white bread. It was Sarah who noticed it. "Whatever is meant to be eating this bread must be nocturnal. It's still here." She pointed to the path.

"Hey, we can follow this. It might show us where the 'Bread Man' lives." Matt grinned.

"Why would we want to know where he lives?" Sarah asked in surprise. "Besides, it looks like he ran out of bread at this point."

Their flat was only a few minutes from the park. They were discussing whether to get a takeaway from the local Chinese when they passed number 102. Both stopped suddenly.

Number 102 was the largest property in their row, still a detached house not yet converted to apartments. They only knew the occupants slightly. The husband left with suit and briefcase every morning at the same time as Matt. They nodded to each other every day. There were two children, a girl and a boy, aged about 11 and 7. The wife seemed to go out quite a bit in the evening, but was at home during the day. You could always tell when she was out because the children cried a lot. Sarah had commented on this more than once, whether the wife would go out so often if she knew how much her children missed her. Matt joked, in his usual manner, that the mother was probably a prostitute and needed the money to pay the mortgage. Sarah had managed to hit him that time, although she conceded he might be right about the size of the family's mortgage.

Today, No. 102 was surrounded by police cars. The front door was open, but it was hardly a security risk.

Sarah counted three policemen in the driveway and another in the hall. A WPC was near her patrol car when Matt and Sarah passed.

Sarah paused, curious. "Is everything ok?" she asked.

"Do you live near here?" the WPC asked.

"Yes, a few doors down, at no. 108" Matt replied, for once entirely serious.

"Have you been out all day?"

"Since 11.30 this morning," Sarah confirmed. "We went to the Boar's Head for lunch and then to the park. What's the problem?" She was quite alarmed by now. It wasn't just the large police presence that worried her, but the way their questions had been met with further queries in reply.

"Do you know the children who live here? Would you recognise them?" the WPC continued.

It was Matt who replied this time. "We know them by sight, but I have no idea what they're called. Why?" He hoped that by adding a question of his own, he might get some answers.

"I'm afraid the little boy has gone missing. No one has seen him since three this afternoon. He was playing in the garden with his sister, and she says she doesn't know where he went. Have you seen anything or anyone suspicious this afternoon?" The WPC had her notebook out now.

Sarah glanced quickly at Matt, but he just shrugged. "No, I'm afraid not," he replied. "We'll keep an eye open for him though. If you're setting up a search, let me know. I'll join straight away."

"That's very kind of you, sir" the WPC smiled with a sudden increase in politeness.

That night, Sarah and Matt sat in their small kitchen looking at each other over their takeaway. Sarah didn't feel hungry. She was thinking about the poor little boy and what his family must be going through. She was also worried about Matt. She'd been certain he was joking about the 'Bread Man' but expected him to mention his concerns to the WPC. Now she wasn't sure whether his silence was a good or bad thing.

Earlier, Matt had gone out with a few of the guys he knew from the Boar's Head. They'd searched the park, particularly any buildings a boy might shelter in, but had no success. A silver mist was developing, smothering the streets as Matt returned, disappointed.

Sarah was sad. Her memory of the little boy was of a lively blond child, quite tall for his age. She really didn't see how that old guy with his stick could kidnap a child. That was presuming he was indeed old. Thinking back, Sarah realised the 'Bread Man' hadn't actually been leaning on his stick; he was simply carrying it. She chastised herself for being worse than Matt, but still didn't sleep well that night.

She was vaguely aware of voices when she awoke around nine. To her surprise Matt was already up. It was unusual for him to get up before ten on a Sunday. She found him in the lounge.

"You look tired," Matt said. "I didn't sleep well last night. Sorry if I disturbed you."

"That's alright, I spent most of the night tossing and

turning myself." Sarah sat next to him on the sofa. "What's up?" she asked. "You look like you've seen a ghost."

"No ghosts, just more bad news" Matt grimaced. "There's no easy way to say this: you just missed the police. They're doing a house-to-house search. It's the little girl who's gone missing now."

"What little girl?" Sarah's brain was struggling to wake up.

"The one from No. 102. First it was the boy yesterday, now his sister is missing," Matt explained. He held her hands in his. "The police say the parents put the girl to bed last night. The father went out quite late to look for their son. The mother was calling all the little boy's friends to see if he was at their house. When the dad got back, the girl's room was empty. The mother is distraught, blaming herself. No one knows if the girl got up and walked out. It's possible someone went into the house to get her."

Sarah's mind was whirling. Why would anyone want to kidnap two children from the same family? Wouldn't it be a huge risk, going to the house to get the daughter when everyone was looking for the son? Or was this extreme confidence; knowing that people were distracted by the missing boy, making the girl easy prey?

No, Sarah thought. The more obvious explanation is that the boy wandered off and got lost and now his sister's gone looking for him and also got lost. But that was just as ridiculous, Sarah admitted. Why would the girl wait until it was dark to look for her brother, and why didn't she go with her father? Could an eleven-year-old really get lost in the neighbourhood she'd lived in all her life?

"Is there a search?" Sarah asked. "Can we join in?"

"I don't know," Matt replied, "but I think I'll pop to the Boar's Head to find out. Have a bath or a coffee to make yourself feel better. I won't be out long."

"Ok" Sarah agreed. "I'm doing roast pork tonight, so if you want to get a snack at the pub with whoever's there, that's fine. I have salad stuff here for me and I know how much you hate salad." She tried to smile. "Just be back for eight please."

Matt squeezed her hand and kissed her forehead. He was gone all day.

...

They were waiting in the park, near the pond, as quietly as they could. Matt could hear his heart beating. He could even hear the hearts of the guys either side of him. He wasn't sure who they were. Quite a crowd had gathered in the Boar's Head that lunchtime.

It was only dusk, but the shade of the sweet-chestnut trees made it darker. Last night's mist had returned, hovering like a silver shroud. There was no way they would be seen behind the rhododendrons next to the pond. His only concern was whether they would miss their target in the gathering gloom. Maybe the 'Bread Man' wouldn't come this way. Maybe he'd already gone home.

They heard the rustle of the plastic carrier bag before they saw him. In an instant they were on him. Matt would never remember afterwards how many of them there were. He could try to blame the five pints, but the truth was that he'd planned this before he'd even got to the pub. It wasn't at all hard to persuade the others that he was right.

It wasn't Matt's fault things got out of hand. His plan was to beat the 'Bread Man' just enough to make him confess where he'd hidden the children. But in the gloom, it was hard to see what was happening. He took aim with his right foot and to his horror heard a sickening crunch. He wasn't the only one to land a kick, and he certainly wasn't the last. At the end, they had to pull someone away to stop him kicking and punching the inert figure on the ground.

They ran as hard as they could, each heading their separate way. Matt stopped running when he was out of the park. He felt as if he'd failed. He had no more idea now where the two kids were than before. And now he couldn't even trail the 'Bread Man' to see if the children were at his home.

He was breathing hard and probably looked a mess. He didn't dare go home. If Sarah thought he'd been fighting at the pub again, she'd kick him out for sure. Nor could he risk walking past No. 102 in case the police were still there. Thinking furiously, Matt walked round the block. He realised he could get to the rear of their flat without being seen.

Quietly he unlocked the back door and went straight

to their bathroom. His reflection in the mirror wasn't as bad as he'd feared. He wasn't scratched or injured. He wasn't covered in blood. His trainers and socks looked a bit the worse for wear, but that was it. Taking them off he stuffed them in the washing machine. For the first time, he was glad he and Sarah had to combine their bathroom and laundry to save space.

To his surprise, when he walked into the lounge, he found Sarah speaking to one of the neighbours; Annie, the Inspector's Widow, who lived over the road. He tried to retreat but it was too late. Sarah called him back in.

"Matt, you must listen to this!" she called. "Annie's just come round. She has some amazing news."

Curious, but with a sinking feeling, Matt walked back into the room. It wasn't possible for Annie to know what had happened, was it? He knew her house backed on to the park but was sure her garden was nowhere near the ornamental pond.

"Hello Matt." Annie smiled. Matt managed to smile back and lowered himself into the spare armchair.

"Go on, Annie," Sarah urged. "Why don't you start again so that Matt can hear everything from the beginning."

"It's about those missing children," Annie explained. "They've both been found safe and well."

Relief flooded through Matt. "That's great!" he said and meant it. "Where were they?"

"At a house on the other side of the park, owned by an elderly couple. You may know them, the Shahs."

"I'm afraid not" Matt said, "but why were they at

the Shahs' house?"

"Sure, you know him," Sarah interrupted. "Mr Shah is the man you keep seeing in the park with the bag of bread for the birds. We saw him yesterday. You call him the 'Bread Man'."

Matt was confused. He felt vindicated to hear that the children had been kidnapped by the 'Bread Man'. He'd known it all along, but he'd never thought that there might be a 'Mrs Bread Man'. He didn't trust himself to speak, but it wasn't a problem. Annie was in full flow.

"The police came round half an hour ago. They knew my Bert, so they popped in to have a chat. They told me the whole story." Annie stopped long enough to take a slurp of tea and then carried on. "I thought at first Mr and Mrs Shah must have kidnapped the children, but it was nothing of the sort. The kids went to them and asked to stay there. The girl left her brother there yesterday and went home for some of their things. Then she snuck out later and joined him. Apparently, Mr and Mrs Shah weren't aware the children had been reported missing. They only found that out this evening. Mr Shah said he was going to their parents to let them know the children were safe but whether he did or not, I don't know. I haven't seen him, but it doesn't matter as Mrs Shah rang the police."

"But why on earth did the children want to stay with Mr & Mrs Shah?" Matt demanded.

"This is the really sad bit," Annie replied. "Mrs Shah's a dinner lady at the local school, so she's got to know

Henrietta quite well."

"She's the girl who went missing from No. 102" Sarah explained to Matt. "The boy is called William."

"Quite so, dear" Anne continued. "Well, young Henrietta formed quite a friendship with Mrs Shah, so when she was looking for a place for her and William to stay, she asked her. Mrs Shah was happy to help, although as I said, she thought Henrietta had told her parents. The girl probably pretended she had permission."

"But why would Henrietta want Mrs Shah to take her and her brother in?" Matt was insistent, his voice getting louder. Sarah threw him a warning glance. She didn't need to say, 'Have you drunk too much?' It was written all over her face. Matt attempted a smile at Annie, but she didn't need any encouragement.

"I was trying to tell you. It seems that poor William and Henrietta are being abused by their father when their mother's out. He's been arrested, you know. It seems he was quite clever not to leave any marks that could be seen, but that whenever his wife was out at her evening class, he laid into the little ones. I'm surprised you didn't hear anything."

It was Sarah who finally managed to reply. "We did hear the kids crying when their mother was out, but we thought they just missed her. We had no idea the father was beating them up."

"The neighbours the other side said the same," Annie sighed. "It's just a shame that no one thought to mention this to the mother, or she might have found out earlier. Although you do wonder how she missed seeing any signs. Still, she claims she knew nothing about it and is insisting the police lock her husband away for a very long time." Annie drank her tea again. "Apparently the mother was about to go on a week's trip with her evening class (she teaches Spanish by the way), and little Henrietta wanted to protect her brother. I guess it's a good thing the kids had Mr & Mrs Shah to go to rather than just running away."

Matt knocked the coffee table over as he jumped up, retching. As he ran to the bathroom, he heard the clatter of the broken tea set and Sarah's indignant cry.

Cavern

Before the hills grew smooth, I existed. For a hundred thousand years of your time - measureless in mine - water trickled downwards. As it passed, it carved my caverns. Then, one waking, the rock beneath me moved and my ways grew deep.

I became a place of silences and sanctuary. In me, summer and winter merged to an even coolness. My waters were fresh. The great gash of my entrance gave shelter.

Bats found me first. In clouds as black as my walls, they flew between me and the forests. Creeping things appeared too, blind worms in my mud. Ferns began to grow in my entrance, and along the gaps where light filtered from above. Soon the big cats discovered me. For centuries I watched their young at play. Then came the bears, lumbering into my passageways, as deep as they dared.

Finally, creatures on two legs appeared. They climbed up from the valley and cowered in my entrance, wrapped in borrowed skins. My shelter pleased them. When their predators had gone they stayed, lighting fires that kept us both warm. Sometimes they would put their hands in the yellow mud and press their palms against my walls; to leave their mark they told me, and to honour my spirit. I needed no such flattery. Beyond feeling, I watched as their young strayed into my chasms. I would hear them calling, and wonder why they could not fly like the bats.

Later, other two-legged creatures came. These people knew colours and lines, and how to make dull rock glow. Wanting to please me, they decorated my sides. Their magic brought the animals I had sheltered onto my walls: tigers and bears, horses, even birds. One young female could draw reindeer as if they pranced before her. The other painters would stop to watch, or bring her gifts of water and coloured clay. She would draw strange creatures too, from the world outside I had never seen: animals with slender necks or huge shaggy bodies. As each one came alive, her companions would dance towards it, spears raised as if to kill, but she would not join them. For her, the pleasure was in the drawing itself.

I cannot remember when the painters left. A storm raged above me, and water gushed down through my rocks. Though the flood drained away, it left pools along my paths. A new stream flowed through me, sometimes a trickle, sometimes a raging torrent. For years my caves were silent again, but for the steady drip drip of water.

Outside, the light came and went. I dozed and woke, and dozed again. Each waking, the forests on the valley sides were thinner, the cries of bird and creature fainter.

The hills grew bare, home only to woolly creatures that bleated. They sheltered under my canopy but gave nothing in return.

By then the two-legged painters lived with these animals. They liked to sit just inside me, eating the food they had brought. I began to understand their babble. They called themselves 'men' and 'women' and spoke as if they ruled the valley. Yet they were afraid of me. Some did enter, but they wished only to mate. Few explored my chambers. They were lucky to return. Parties of men with loud voices have come here several times, searching for some foolish youth lost within me. My silences should have warned them.

Again the light came and went over the valley. There were new sounds, distant thumps as of rock falling into sand, or a puffing that travelled up and down. With them came many new visitors. They peered into my opening and shouted to the echo, as irritating as a plague of insects.

Last wakening, different men came, stronger and quieter, showing no fear. They carried lights on their heads and knew how to crawl or wade through my tunnels. As they explored, they gave names to each of my features, as if they were the first to discover me. I listened to their conceit, and could not determine whether they came to hide or breed.

Suddenly, two of these people stumbled into my innermost cavern. They crouched in silence, looking upwards. One shone a light around my walls. He saw the paintings above him. "Tom!" he shouted.

"Oh, my God!"

Their voices echoed. For the first time since the painters left, I heard myself revered.

Finally they turned to leave. "We must tell Lee!" Tom said.

"No!" the other shouted back. "He'll have the Press in before you know it. Let's keep this to ourselves."

"Don't be stupid! This place will make us!"

Then they were gone.

Later - it seemed just a little while - the men returned. They brought another man and an older woman, weaker specimens who needed help through my narrow ways. It took them a long time to struggle into my cavern. Standing beside the stream, they flashed their lights above them, backwards and forwards. Crying out in amazement they marvelled at so much darkness, so many deer and horses rushing through it. When they spoke, it was with joy.

"Let's get a closer look!" Tom said.

They had carried bundles through my waters, and they opened the wrappings. Inside were rods that they attached to the rocks. The man they called Dan seemed to be their leader. When he was satisfied, they fixed lights back onto their heads and began to climb. Painfully, slowly, as if weighed down by their clothing, they edged upwards. I did not understand why they found it so difficult. The people who painted the shapes they sought were not afraid of my darkness, nor of the height.

Finally, they hauled themselves over the last rocks, and stood where the reindeer woman had stood. At first they seemed dumb or sleeping. When at last they woke, each spoke in a hushed voice.

"Incredible!" the woman whispered. She shone her light onto the rock. A sabre-toothed tiger flickered back. "One on top of the other…"

"Are they as old as they look, Professor?" the younger man asked her. He seemed excited, like the dancers who waved their spears.

"These have been here twenty thousand years, Lee. At least."

The young man began to laugh. "Bingo!" he said.

"Don't talk like that," the woman replied. "This is a sacred place."

"You don't believe that stuff, do you?" Tom mocked. "These paintings will make our reputations! Yours included!"

"Only if you keep them secret," Lee warned. "Or Jack's lot will get in first. We need a camera crew down here tomorrow."

The leader turned away. His face bore the expression humans call anger, but he said nothing.

Going nearer him, the woman stood looking at the paintings. "I've dreamt all my life of finding somewhere like this," she said. "But now I feel guilty. Even our breath will damage them."

"I told Tom that," he replied. "He wouldn't listen. Too many pound signs."

The other men were talking loudly, fetching baggage up and down and flashing lights onto my sides. Reindeer and bear appeared, then vanished into night, only to appear again. I became weary of their voices. It was time for them to leave but they did not. They made me hot with their lights, and their comings and goings irritated me. They were like the dung flies that swarmed around my entrance.

So I stretched and let the cooling stream flow through my channels.

Crying out, the woman turned. "The stream's rising," she called. "It must be raining up top."

"Just a shower," Tom replied. "No need to panic. The forecast was dry."

"That stream's definitely rising," Dan said. "We must go." He gathered his baggage.

The other men lingered on the ledge. "I'll just take a few more shots," Lee called.

"There isn't time!" Dan shouted. "I'm going - even if you aren't."

"Wait for me," the woman called. They slithered down together urgently, towards the gap where they had entered.

I let them go. Their lamps flickered as they scrambled over the rocks and into the darkness.

"We need to convince the money men," Lee said, squatting down and pointing some object at my wall. His voice echoed around my vastness, like an insect's buzz. He annoyed me, yet still he lingered, making clicking sounds and flashing lights.

So I stretched again. Water gushed through my veins.

"Come on!" Tom shouted. "Or we'll get trapped!"

They began to panic, sliding down my rocks in a

maddened flight. Crying out in pain they fell and scrambled up again. Together they began to wade the stream. It was up to their waists. One fell. He grabbed at the other man, until they both fell. Their lights shone briefly through the water, passing under the roof of the channel. Then they went out.

For a long time I have waited for someone to return. They do not come. In the silence drops fall gently from my roof, with the rhythm of ages.

Tie a Red Ribbon

———

Notes of first interview with Jonathan Fallon, lawyer, aged 29.

"I know it sounds a bit odd: not to have noticed earlier. But I wasn't expecting it. They didn't include it in the sales particulars. Can you imagine? 'For Sale: beautiful two bed-flat in converted mansion. Own ghost'. If they'd told me it was haunted, I wouldn't have gone anywhere near. Although it wasn't too bad at first. After all, how many ghosts clean up after you?

It's the first time I've had my own place. The flats are small so there isn't much room, and I like to keep things tidy. Like I said, I didn't notice anything odd initially. Then I came home late one evening, absolutely soaked. It hadn't been raining when I left the guys in the pub, and I didn't have a brolly with me. It was cold too. I remember feeling shivery when I got home.

Fortunately, there's lino in the entrance hall but even so I'd left muddy footprints all the way to the bathroom. I couldn't face tidying up until I'd defrosted, so I threw my wet clothes on the floor and had a shower. I was in there a little while, perhaps half an hour. I felt much warmer afterwards. I pulled on an old tracksuit and went to tidy up. That was when I first noticed.

I could have sworn I'd left my clothes in a heap near the shower, but they weren't there. I searched the bathroom, but they were nowhere to be seen. I went to make a cup of tea, but I was even more bewildered when I found the washing machine on in the kitchen, my clothes tumbling round. The machine was half-way through its cycle, so it must have started shortly after I'd got in. Believe me, I know I didn't take my clothes off in the kitchen, put them in the machine and then walk naked to the shower.

I was trying to fathom it out when I looked back to the hallway. I stopped in surprise. My muddy footprints had been mopped up. The floor was slightly wet, the mop and bucket in the corner. I put my hand in the bucket and felt the water; it was still warm. So now you're asking me to believe that I mopped the floor while I was naked, before I got in the shower? There's no way I could have forgotten doing that!

I put the mop away and sat in the lounge, staring at the door. I don't know what or who I thought I'd see. I think I was hoping that Maureen from next door had popped in, seen the mess, and taken pity on me. She's a sweet old thing, so I can just see her trying to be helpful. There's only one snag, or rather two. First, she hasn't got a key; at least I've never given her one. And second, there's no way she'd have been able to reach the bucket on top of the kitchen cupboard: she's far too short.

I decided to go round to see Maureen anyway. I made myself a bit more presentable and took some nice biscuits. I figured that if I did owe her a big 'thank you', I could leave the biscuits as a present. I was also planning to ask her to knock next time, rather than letting herself into my flat. I have to have some privacy after all. In fact, I was wondering whether it would be too rude to change the locks.

Maureen took a little while to answer the door. "Can I have a word?" I asked her.

"Hello, Jon, nice to see you. Yes of course," she replied. "What can I do for you?"

I decided to chance it, so I went straight ahead and thanked her for tidying up for me. Her face answered my question. She clearly hadn't been anywhere near my flat. I wasn't counting on the violence of her response though. She shrieked, pushed me backwards and slammed the door in my face. I was absolutely astonished.

I knocked again, but she was ignoring me. I felt a bit of a chump hammering on her door, so I went back to my flat. I decided to have an early night and hope that things would be clearer the next day.

It was a Saturday, and I was having a lie in when I heard a knock on the door. Pulling on my dressing gown, I opened it to find Maureen staring at me.

"Oh, Jon," she said, "I feel so bad about yesterday. Please forgive me."

"That's no problem," I replied, letting her in.

I was expecting to have to tell her all about what had happened but, strangely, she seemed to know.

"How long has it been going on?" she asked.

"Do you mean the 'phantom cleaner of old Melrose Hall'?" I was feeling more good-humoured by now. I was even beginning to see the funny side. Maureen clearly didn't.

"That's exactly what I mean," she said. "I need to know when it started."

"Well last night was the first and only time that I'm aware of," I answered. Her sombre manner was starting to get to me.

"Are you sure? Have you had anything similar before?" She was insistent.

"No, I'm sure. Except," I added, "a couple of times my keys have mysteriously appeared on the hook by the door, and I've absolutely no memory of putting them there. But that's probably just me forgetting things." I tried to reassure her.

"I'm afraid not." Maureen was quite firm. "It means he's back. He never could stand mess, apparently, so now he tidies up for people, whether they like it or not."

"Who does?" I asked. I wasn't quite sure whether Maureen was pulling my leg. It would be a great wind-up. I'd figured Maureen was far too strait-laced (and dare I say it too old?) to dream up an elaborate joke.

"I'm only going on what others have told me," she insisted. "He was the old lord of this house, before they turned it into flats. He must have died horribly to be so tied to this place. Sometimes he's quiet; then other times he's everywhere. I've no idea why. Maybe something triggers him off."

"Well, I hope it wasn't my dirty footprints that got him going," I protested. "After all, if you can't make mess in your own flat, there's something wrong with the world."

Maureen cut me off. "That's what I'm telling you. As far as he's concerned, this isn't your flat, it still belongs to him. If you're neat and tidy, all's well. Just don't make mess and whatever you do, don't have any parties here. He absolutely hates parties. I remember what happened last time." She was shivering.

I wanted to hug Maureen, to tell her everything would be ok, but wasn't sure that would be right. She was old enough to be my granny. I decided not to tell her that I'd arranged a flat-warming party the following weekend. Hopefully by then, things would have gone back to normal.

"Where are my manners?" I suddenly remembered. "Do you want a cup of tea? I still have those biscuits."

"That would be lovely." Maureen actually smiled.

I stood and walked into the kitchen, smiling back. My smile froze on my face. The kettle was just reaching boiling point. A plate of biscuits and two cups had been neatly laid out, next to a tea pot, all on a little tray that I didn't even know I owned. I poured the hot water into the teapot and carried the tray through.

"That was quick," Maureen noted. I didn't have the heart to tell her why.

Nothing else happened that week. I made sure I did the washing up immediately after each meal. I even dried up, instead of my usual trick of letting things drain. I guess I was hoping that if I kept my nose (and my flat) clean the entire week, I might be forgiven for the small party on Saturday. I certainly wasn't going to cancel it. There was no way I was running scared from a ghost, even if he was the landlord from hell.

The party wasn't that loud; really it wasn't. I'd invited my mum, so it was never going to be an orgy. We put a bit of music on, but I told everyone my neighbour was elderly and we kept the volume down. There were a few beer cans and bottles. We put these in the recycling straight away. My mum even did the washing up before she went home. All in all, it was a pretty tame affair. I was even teased for having grown up, now I had my own place.

I woke late on Sunday. I didn't think I'd drunk that much but my head said otherwise: I could feel a steady dull thumping. It took me a little while to realise the thumping was coming from my front door. Gingerly I rose and made my way down the hallway. It was Maureen.

"I can't believe you ignored me," she was almost shouting. At first, I couldn't work out what she meant. Then it came to me.

"Look," I replied, "we were quiet. There's no mess and no harm done."

"You don't understand," she insisted. "it's not just the mess. He can't stand music and laughter."

"We were quiet," I insisted. "Surely you're not telling me I can never have people round to my flat?"

"I've told you, it's not your flat as far as he's concerned. He may never forgive you," Maureen insisted grimly. "Let's hope it doesn't get any worse. Just keep an eye open for red ribbons."

"What?"

"You'll see them. Little pieces of red ribbon tied to trees or gate posts."

"And what exactly do these pieces of red ribbon signify?" My voice was getting higher, incredulous.

"Don't shout at me!" Maureen shouted back. "Something terrible always happens when a red ribbon appears." She stormed off towards her flat.

Bewildered, I shut the door and had a look around. I couldn't see any trace of red ribbons. I told myself I was being silly and made a strong coffee and some toast. Perhaps Maureen was starting to lose it? I'd heard somewhere that paranoia can be a sign of dementia.

To be honest, I thought nothing more about it that day. I didn't see Maureen and presumed she was avoiding me. I slept badly that night though. I kept dreaming of red ribbons, fluttering in the night breeze. I saw one on a wrought iron gate and another on a little bay tree. There was a third on an ornamental light near a gravel driveway. I was exhausted when the alarm woke me on Monday.

It's always hard to work when you're shattered, and I found that Monday particularly difficult. I just about managed to get through it thanks to large doses of caffeine and chocolate biscuits. I left as early as I could. Fortunately, my boss was away so I didn't have to do the usual macho 'who can stay longest in the office' routine. I figured if I could get a decent night's sleep,

I'd be as right as rain the next day.

I was walking home in a bit of a daze when I noticed the ambulance. It had stopped in front of one of the larger houses that back onto the park. I wasn't being nosey; it's just that I had to stop to let the paramedics past. They had a guy on a stretcher, and he didn't look good. His face was a strange grey colour.

"Heart attack," a voice said behind me. I turned and saw what I presumed was a neighbour.

"Unexpected?" I asked back.

"'Fraid so and he's only 37."

I looked back in astonishment. The pallid face looked way older than that. I guess a heart attack will age anyone.

I was walking away when I saw it. It stopped me dead in my tracks. There was the little red ribbon, tied to a small light next to the drive. It looked for all the world like one of the ribbons from my dream. I pretty much sprinted home and barricaded myself in. I wasn't in the mood for talking to anyone that evening. I slept badly again, but luckily I didn't dream of any red ribbons.

Tuesday was slightly warmer and brighter, so I felt a bit better going to work that day. I'd almost reached the train station when I saw the ribbon. Its bright red was a stark contrast to the black gate it was tied to. The gate and house behind it looked familiar. Then I remembered; I'd also seen this ribbon in my nightmare on Sunday.

I didn't quite know what to do. It felt wrong to carry on, but I could hardly go up to the door, ring the bell and ask total strangers if everything was ok. I was still dithering when the burglar alarm suddenly went off. I knew I couldn't ignore this. I opened the gate and walked to the front door. I found the door slightly open.

I knew not to march straight in, I am a lawyer after all. I rang 999 on my mobile and reported the break in. Then I pulled my gloves on and gently pushed open the door. That was when I saw him. He was an elderly gentleman, in his pyjamas. He was lying prone on the floor at the foot of the stairs. I didn't need to go any closer to see he was dead. His head was pointing in completely the wrong direction. He must have heard burglars in the middle of the night and tripped as he went down the stairs to investigate.

There was no way I could go into work that day. I called in to explain the situation and was surprised to find my boss was quite sympathetic. He told me to take the rest of the day off and, indeed, the rest of the week if I needed it.

I was glad I hadn't gone into the house: it made it much easier to persuade the police that I'd had nothing to do with the break in. They were a little surprised that the burglar alarm had gone off when there was no sign of the burglars. I figured maybe the wind had moved the front door slightly, triggering the alarm again. I didn't mention the red ribbon. They would never have believed me.

I pottered around my flat for the rest of the day, catching up on some chores I'd been meaning to do. I hoped my devilish landlord would be happy. Sadly I, was wrong; very wrong.

I hadn't seen Maureen since Sunday morning. I hadn't thought anything of it at first. By Tuesday evening I was wondering if I ought to check whether she was ok. I knew that Tuesdays she usually had a friend round to play bridge. I'd teased her about him before, calling him her 'fancy man'. She hadn't seemed to mind so maybe I wasn't that far off the mark. I heard him arrive at seven as usual but was astonished to find him still in the corridor ten minutes later when I went to put my bin out.

"Isn't she in?" I asked, surprised.

"I can't get any answer. Have you seen her today?"

"I'm afraid I haven't seen her since Sunday morning," I replied, wishing I'd done something about it already.

I walked over to him. Maureen's fancy man was a small wiry fellow, probably in his 80s but well preserved. He still had a fine head of grey hair, or a very good wig. He was around half my height.

"I think she keeps a spare key under the pot plant there," he said.

I turned to look at where he was pointing and had a shock. The plant was a beautiful little bay tree. A small red ribbon was attached to it, just as in my dream. With a sense of dread, I lifted the pot and found the key. I handed it over. I didn't want to be the first in her flat.

We stood in her hallway, our eyes adjusting to the gloom. I tried the light switch, but it didn't work. I wondered about going back to my flat for a torch, but we could just about see. The curtains weren't drawn, and a pale orange glow shone into the flat from the nearby streetlight.

The flat felt cold and barren, as if no one had been in the apartment for months. There was a layer of dust on the radiator in the hallway. I couldn't imagine Maureen letting her place get dirty, even if we didn't have a ghostly landlord cleaning up for us.

Although I'd never been in Maureen's flat before, its layout was similar to mine. We found nothing in the kitchen or lounge. I glanced into the bathroom but that was empty too. The bedroom door was closed. I opened it slowly and peered into the darkened room. Here the curtains were drawn but not quite fully. A sliver of light was penetrating the gloom, across the floor and over the bed. My eyes followed it from the window. I recoiled at the sight in front of me.

For the first time I noticed the dreadful smell. Maureen was in bed, as if asleep. One glance was enough though. I could see clearly that she was no longer with us. Her glassy eyes were staring at the door, straight through me. She looked like she'd been dead for months.

I didn't enter the room and turned to see if Maureen's fancy man was ok. He was nowhere to be seen. So, I went back into the hallway, but he'd clearly scarpered. I picked up the phone to ring the police. The line was dead. I had to go back to my flat to make the call.

Now, I can see why the police found it all too much of a coincidence. First, I call them to say I've found a dead guy in his burgled house, then that evening I'm calling them to report finding my neighbour dead in her bed. They were very professional though. They never once voiced their suspicions, but I knew what they were thinking. I told them everything, right from hearing Maureen's fancy man knocking on her door. The only thing I didn't mention was the red ribbon on the bay tree. I just felt that would complicate things. In fact, you're the first person I've told about the ribbons and my dream.

I've felt my grip on reality slipping a bit since then, to be honest. I didn't go to the office that week. Actually, I've not been back at all. The firm's medic signed me off as unfit to work. They're still paying me, so I'm not going to complain. I just don't understand what happened.

First the good news: the post-mortem confirmed that Maureen had died of natural causes, so there's no way I could have bumped her off. But here's the rub. It also determined that she'd died about three months ago. Just before I moved into my flat. That would explain why her power and phone line had been cut off when she didn't pay her bills. I guess she didn't do direct debit.

Now the police tell me Maureen's friend Ken, who matches the description I gave them, died eighteen months ago. Apparently, there's no way I could have seen him at her flat.

Then there's the question of the guy in his pyjamas. Again, I'm in the clear for the death. He'd apparently had a massive aneurism before he fell down the stairs, so he was probably dead before he broke his neck. Someone's been caught trying to sell the stuff they took from his house. So far, so good. But the police can't work out what made me look in the house since there isn't actually a burglar alarm. The box on the outside is a fake. There's no way I could have heard an alarm at that house. So now the police think I'm connected in some way to the gang that robbed the house.

And that's not all. It gets worse. I decided to move out of the flat, sell it to some other poor unsuspecting sucker. I wasn't staying there any longer than I had to, I can tell you. I moved back in with my Mum, well until I came here that is. She's been absolutely great; so supportive.

I was packing up my stuff with my Mum's help. She'd brought round a pile of boxes to load things into. I was going through the drawers in my kitchen when I came across them. I just stood there, staring. There they were, underneath my tea towels: a packet of little red ribbons. I swear I didn't put them there."

Notes of first interview taken by Dr P Barrowclough, Consultant Psychiatrist, Wooding Mental Hospital.

The Deadly Morris Dance

There can't be many company bonding days that end in murder.

The weekend started well. It was a lovely Autumn morning as Tony and I arrived at the Harrogate office. Jenny and Sarah were waiting. Dan from Design turned up soon afterwards. Bill was already waiting for us. With me from IT and Tony from Human Resources, the management team was almost complete. Only Mick from Sales was missing.

Jenny's mouth was set in its usual sour line. "You're late," she called. I bit my tongue and smiled. We were probably being assessed already. Bill pretended to be an easy-going employer, but he was ruthless. If anyone failed to meet his standards, they were out. Starting at the crack of dawn could be our first test.

Mick arrived in a Mercedes, driven by a stunning brunette. "This is Karen," he announced. "She'll be joining us for dinner." He made a big show of kissing her goodbye, no doubt for our benefit, before she sped off. Dan whispered, "I wonder how he got a lift so early?"

and laughed softly.

"What's this one called?" Bill demanded from the doorway. We were used to Mick turning up with his latest date. At the barbeque it was Carol. Irena came to the Christmas meal. We didn't put a name on invitations anymore, just 'Mick Plus One.'

"Karen Fosdyke," Mick announced proudly. Not that her name meant anything to us.

Bill seemed annoyed about something, but his smile soon returned. "Well, good for you," he replied amiably, "she's beautiful. Now let's find our hidden talents."

Everyone nodded vehemently.

The first two activities were quite enjoyable. We started by orienteering in the woods along the Chevin ridge. To our relief, our trail didn't drop down the steep paths towards Otley, but even so we were soon out of breath trying to keep up with Mick. He was very fit. "All that chasing after women," Tony whispered to me. A few moments later Mick slipped on some leaves and fell flat on his back. He had the grace to join in the laughter at his expense. He must have been aching and glad to finish. I know I was. Learning to shoot sounded easier.

It rained a little towards the end of our session at the shooting club, but we hardly noticed. The instructor was fun, and we were soon having a good time. Jenny proved to be the best shot. I'll admit I wondered if she'd been practicing so she could impress Bill. We all knew he was a keen member of a shooting club. I wouldn't have put it past her. She always showed absolute devotion to him – whether real or out of ambition I could never decide.

At twelve we adjourned to Darnley Court for lunch. After eating in the cafe, we trooped across the lobby to the private dining hall. "We're going to learn to Morris Dance," Bill announced.

"I didn't know we'd be dancing." Jenny sounded shocked.

"It's an excellent way of building team spirit," Bill enthused. "Everyone has to play their part, or the dance doesn't work. I've hired an expert to teach us an old English dance. Here he is!"

A newcomer entered the hall. He must have been sixty but looked fitter than all of us. "Afternoon," he said. "My name's Gideon and I'm here to teach you the Donkey Dance. Now, who's volunteering to be the donkey? I've got a genuine nineteenth century head for you to wear." He didn't sound like the country bumpkin we'd expected, more like a retired head teacher.

Everyone looked around, embarrassed. The dining hall was grand, but it was also long and cold. Glass doors faced onto an inner courtyard. None of the ancient windows fitted properly, and with an open door at each end of the hall, there was a fierce draught. I could see a similar room the other side of the courtyard, also with French windows. It looked like a library.

The tables and chairs had been pushed to one side, leaving space for us to practise. I hoped the room would be warmer with the velvet curtains drawn and reaching to the floor. Otherwise, it would be a chilly dinner.

"Come on," Gideon insisted. "It's quite simple. Six of you dance a jig around the donkey. At the end, the donkey runs down the middle and bounces off a trampoline. Here's one I made earlier, as they say." He pulled a small trampoline from the corner. "After dinner tonight, we'll put on a show for your partners and colleagues. I'll announce that you're entertaining them, so you'll have to learn how to do it, won't you?"

"Blackmail!" Dan pointed out. We all laughed, but no one stepped forward.

"All right. I'll wear the Donkey head," Bill said. "Then at least we'll get started." It was a big, heavy thing. When it was on, his face was completely hidden. He looked like Bottom in 'Midsummer's Night Dream', but we didn't dare laugh.

All afternoon we learnt the dance, getting hot and tired. At first the jig was more like a scrum, but by the fifth attempt we'd got the idea. Bill was surprisingly fit, despite his ample midriff. Though he puffed and landed heavily, he became quite good at running up the hall and jumping off the trampoline with a flourish. There was a lot of shared laughter and banter. Even Jenny joined in. We were indeed bonding.

"Now for your gear," Gideon said, fetching a large basket. He took out a supply of white shirts, black trousers and black shoes, each carefully named. "Bill's PA guessed your sizes. You can swap if necessary. They're all the same. Here are the bells to put around your right leg and left arm." He passed a set to Bill. "And here's your donkey costume," he added, giving him a patchwork tunic to pull over the shirt and trousers.

"Help me put these bells on, Tilly," Tony begged me. "I'm hopeless at this sort of thing."

At seven o'clock the 'other halves' and friends joined us. Dan and I had finally admitted we were more than 'just' colleagues and asked to sit at the same table. Neither of us wanted to make polite conversation with a guest; nor were we bothered by the prospect of office chatter.

After an excellent meal, everyone waited expectantly. The waitresses stood in front of the doors to prevent interruptions. With the curtains pulled across the French doors and candles on the tables, the room looked quite cosy.

As the dance was short, we'd decided to do it three times. Between each Donkey bounce, Gideon would perform a sword dance of his own. At first all went as planned. We did the jig; the Donkey ran down the middle, launched onto the trampoline, boing, then landed on both feet. Gideon followed with an amazing sword dance. Everyone was watching and clapping when Tony whispered, "One of us is missing." Urgently we looked round. It was Dan. We were about to take our positions for the second Donkey Dance and Dan had disappeared. Sarah swore. "Probably gone for a smoke," she said caustically. I recalled a waitress relighting the candles on one of the tables. A draught must have blown them out when Dan slipped outside. I was furious.

All we could do was rope Gideon in to take his place. Luckily the dance went well again. The Donkey skipped down the middle, jumped onto the trampoline, twang, then landed lightly on one foot. Gideon did an even more complicated solo.

By the third Donkey dance, we had six dancers again. Dan was full of apologies. He hadn't realized how short Gideon's sword dance was and had popped out for a smoke. "Idiot!" Jenny hissed. For once I agreed with her.

We did the final dance with Gideon watching from the side. The Donkey ran down the middle to the trampoline, launched himself with a boing, and landed to tremendous applause. He was the boss after all. Even our guests felt obliged to congratulate him.

They were still applauding when we heard the most appalling scream from the other side of the courtyard. I shall never forget it. One of the waitresses had found Karen Fosdyke's body in the library. She was shaking and sobbing when she ran into the hall. "I didn't do it! I didn't do it!" she kept crying, wringing her apron in her hands. "She was on the floor when I went in. Poor, poor lady…"

It was chaos after that. Everyone ran to the exits to see what had happened. Jenny and I headed for the far door knowing it led to the lobby, but we were turned back by a waitress. I tripped over the trampoline, almost falling flat on my face. Pushing myself back up, I saw there was mud on my hands. In the way that you fix on a silly detail in a crisis, I wondered how it had got there.

After that, the police arrived. We didn't know Karen. Mick had only been dating her a few weeks. But it was awful to think of her being murdered. Sarah and Jenny started crying and I couldn't stop shivering. The poor woman had been stabbed with one of the steak knives from dinner. The knife was still in her back.

Our guests were sent home, with names and addresses noted, but we were detained. We weren't even allowed to talk to each other. That was when we realized we were suspects.

For hours we sat in miserable silence as each of us was called into the manager's office and questioned. Though it was only October, the nights were getting cold and by now it was well after midnight. My mind kept going round and round. It was the proverbial bad dream. How could one of us have killed Mick's girlfriend? We had all been dancing. It must have been an outsider. Yet the staff insisted no one could have entered the building. The outer doors were locked and there was a receptionist in the foyer. Everyone else was watching us. Jenny might have had a motive: jealousy perhaps or wanting to protect Bill in some way. But she'd never been out of my sight, other than when she went to the Ladies room. Could she have got round to the library in that time?

I've always liked solving puzzles. I suppose that's why I work in IT. To keep calm, I started to go over what had happened. Karen's body was found in the library, which ran parallel to the hall. You could get to it by leaving the hall through the North door and going through the lobby. I hadn't noticed Karen go out, but I was getting ready for our dance and not watching the guests. No one could have gone that way after the dancing started, without being spotted. There was another route however: through the glass doors, across the courtyard and into the French windows opposite. Our windows were hidden behind curtains, so perhaps someone could have sneaked out. But no one could have done that without disturbing our dance. Except Dan. In horror, I realized that Dan must be prime suspect. He was the only one who'd left while we were performing. No wonder he'd been with the police so long. I couldn't believe Dan would kill anyone, much less Karen. He'd only met her today. Besides, he hadn't been gone that long.

Then I recalled the candles blowing out. Maybe the French doors had been opened by someone other than Dan? The courtyard was paved but not particularly well: it was muddy in parts. And there was mud on the floor. Or was it on the trampoline?

I couldn't help it. I looked up sharply towards Bill. He was sitting in the far corner, well away from us. Our eyes made contact and I felt a chill pass through me. Quickly I lowered my eyes. I couldn't be right. Bill was dancing the whole time. Besides, what motive would he have? He didn't know Karen was coming. None of us did until Mick introduced her. So, if someone wanted to kill her, it couldn't have been planned in advance.

My mind was racing. The Donkey Dance would have been the perfect cover. Bill could have slipped behind the curtain to the French windows while Gideon did his sword dance. There were differences in the three dances. The first and third time, the Donkey sounded heavy. The second time, he seemed lighter and made more of it: he skipped. The enormity of what I was thinking made me feel sick. Dan was much lighter than Bill. What if Bill swapped with him? That would have given Bill time to sneak out. Maybe Bill said it was a joke, or that he was tired. Dan would do whatever the Boss asked. No one would have noticed with the tunic hiding the Donkey's body.

My theory was growing. Mud on the trampoline could have only got there if the Donkey had gone outside. Bill must have asked Karen to meet him in the library and crept up behind her. Then he returned to do the third dance. "But why should Bill kill Karen?" The question pulled me up short.

He'd seemed annoyed when Mick introduced her. Maybe they'd met before. Then I remembered some office gossip. According to Sarah, Bill had gone to Mauritius to be married but returned single. He'd never mentioned it himself, but Sarah said he'd been stood up at the altar. That was why he was so crochety. His fiancée's name was Karen. Could it be the same woman?

How do you accuse your boss of murder? Dan would never do so but he must by now be realizing he'd been used. If I accused Bill, I could kiss my job goodbye. And I had no real evidence. Yet I had to help Dan.

Feeling weak, I got up and walked towards the policewoman.

For The Children

It was difficult to pack the car in so confined a space, but she daredn't open the garage doors. Though the watch on her home seemed to have been relaxed, someone even now might be snooping, perhaps from one of the windows opposite. Nowadays, neighbours were not to be trusted.

Gasping a little with the weight, Kate lifted the tent and dumped it on top of the case, from where it slid conveniently to the back of the trailer. The air rifle gave the bag an unnatural stiffness but was completely hidden, and the Horlicks and powdered milk tins containing the pellets looked convincing enough, the packing inside preventing any rattling as she picked them up. The blankets and towels were more difficult to pack and reluctantly she was forced to reject the most threadbare, then she stood considering the other items she'd listed as indispensable. Now the actual moment of departure had arrived she realised many were in fact luxuries already - washing up liquid, hand-cream, Brillo pads . . . They'd cost her hours of walking and queuing and extortionate prices on the black market, and would soon be exhausted. Still, she must take some of the more obvious ones, or an alert city guard might become suspicious and insist on a thorough search. That would finish her. Ironically a search was less likely than a few days ago. The authorities would want to keep the traffic moving and do as little as possible to arouse public hostility. After all, apathy had been their best assistant for years.

The children appeared at the back door, excited and quarrelsome at the prospect of an unexpected holiday.

"Can I take Charlie?' Phip asked, his face hidden behind a mound of soft toy.

Marion was holding a saucepan that had been forgotten and, girl-like, trying to look as though she were in command of the situation. Kate's first reaction was to insist that there was no room for anything more, then she relented.

'Just Charlie,' she said. 'But he'll have to sit on your lap.' The children would have little enough to play with.

'We'll put your buckets and spades in after all,' she added.

Small buckets and spades would be useful and it was vital the children should be kept happy. No matter how carefully she might explain the situation to them, they could so easily say or do something to arouse suspicion.

Together they slipped the last of the tins into the trailer and pulled the cover taut. Her head was aching with tiredness and fear, but she smiled and suggested the children pay a last visit to the toilet while she packed the day bag with their drinks and crisps. Finding those packets of crisps had been marvellous good fortune, for they would do more than any grown-up assurance to persuade Phip that life was returning to normal. Mrs Lacey must have had them in her storeroom for nearly a year.

It was dark by the time Kate had finished and she stood for a moment in the garden, looking at the swing they'd made last year, and the apple tree at last about to give fruit. She'd mowed the lawn, on the principle that even nowadays people going on holiday always did so, and it was all so neat, so suburban that she couldn't credit the events of the last months.

She thought of Frank. Even his name was inappropriate. People called Frank didn't get themselves arrested and turned into heroes. Heroes were tall men with names like Titus or Che, not balding little journalists, as terrified as the next man. Her eyes were beginning to sting and she looked back at their home. If Frank were indeed right, that could well be her last sight of the house, and she tried to fix every detail of it upon her memory.

Afterwards she went indoors to check that all the windows and doors were locked securely. Once the looters arrived that would be no protection of course, but Frank might be wrong, after all.

The children were growing impatient and she opened the garage doors. Mrs Jones was putting her milk bottles on the step and called across the japonica.

'You off dear? Are you sure it's wise? The news is

very bad tonight.'

'It's always bad,' Kate replied, a little too brightly. 'I've got the permits, so I might as well use them before they expire.'

'That's true dear. They're hard enough to get now aren't they, and you with poor Frank... how is he by the way? Have you been to see him lately?'

'They let me go last week, but I was only allowed five minutes.'

It was necessary to chat, but irritating, and she glanced down the road to see if the usual car was there. It would be a nuisance if the police decided to follow her and check her route. There was no car that night, however. Every man must be needed.

'Well, I wish you a pleasant journey,' Mrs Jones continued. 'Let's hope the strikes are over by the time you get back.' She lowered her voice. 'Our Bob says there's a lot of tanks about today, so I should watch out for them.'

For an instant Kate felt an urge to warn the older woman, to take her by the shoulders and shout, 'Are you blind? Can't you see what's happening? This isn't like every other strike ...' but she merely smiled. A surprised expression and the advice 'not to let it get you down' would have been the only response, and gossip at her 'strangeness' might result. 'Strange' people soon found themselves of interest to men in fawn uniforms.

And so the farewells were made, and the trailer pushed out onto the road; she never could reverse the car when it was attached. The children settled under the blanket on the back seat, the aspirins she had powdered into their milk beginning to have effect. (That had been another stroke of luck: the milkman returning to work in time for her to give the children a treat at dinner and take two precious bottles with her). Then she checked again that all the necessary papers were in her handbag.

It was nine o'clock by the time she'd driven across the city. There was still a little traffic, despite the general strike, and as Mrs Jones had said, a good deal of troop activity. The children were asleep and she turned the radio on low. Throughout the day she'd avoided the hourly bulletin for fear of frightening them, and the measured seriousness of the news reader's tones disturbed her. Apparently, his instructions had been changed, the cheerful note of the past weeks had become too obviously inappropriate. After various trivialities about sporting events and the weather, he announced that the four pickets sentenced to death under the new Protection of the State Bill had been refused the right to appeal by the Lord Chief Justice's department. It was expected that the sentences would be carried out that night to avoid the danger of demonstrations by left-wing extremists. (Which meant that the sentences had already been carried out, Kate commented mentally.)

The government had appealed for calm, the Prime Minister himself appearing before a large crowd outside the House of Commons that afternoon. In a fine speech he'd outlined the reasons for the Lord Chief Justice's decision, stressing the need for unified action against the small minority trying to destroy British society. An excerpt from his speech followed, climaxed by the usual applause.

The strike was now weakening, the bulletin continued, several small firms reopening and fighting breaking out between strikers and workers wishing to enter a factory in the north. Two men had died and large numbers of arrests had been made. Official sources estimated, in a report out that day, that with the public's co-operation the nation's manufacturing industry could return to normal in six weeks, and martial law could be repealed by the end of the year.

The end of the year? In fury she clicked the radio into silence. She hoped Frank had heard that bit. It would give him a grim satisfaction, though he was too concerned and humane to take much pleasure in having been right.

The thought occurred suddenly that he mightn't be alive and she pulled at her fingernail to drive the fear away. They wouldn't harm him. It would be politically inexpedient, giving the militants another martyr to champion. Alive he was just a foolish journalist with a degree in economics and an interest in futurology. Ten years ago, he had written a best-seller on the possible end of British society. If some bright academic hadn't produced a thesis highlighting the similarity between present events and Frank's analysis, her Frankie would have remained nothing more than a past news item in the public mind.

Yet he had been uncannily right. The lorry drivers' strike coinciding with a miners' dispute and leading to the introduction of a three-day week (more damaging than in the 1970s because it was more extended); a new Middle East war aggravating the already desperate energy crisis; increasing crimes of violence leading to demands for a strengthening of law and order and a publicly welcomed state of repression; inflation at 35% and a declining economy with ten per cent unemployed...

All the ingredients he had suggested were now present, together with an ever-widening gap between unions and management, haves and have-nots, north and south, London and the provinces. A recipe for civil disorder Frank had claimed, sounding a grim warning. He had returned to public notice on television and radio, at student gatherings or CBI conferences, partly (she had to admit) because it paid well, but also out of some sense of mission that had given him a dogged courage which had made his arrest inevitable.

She wondered if he would know where to look for her if he were freed and decided that he would. They had several times discussed their actions should the children seem in danger and had bought the farm with a half joking agreement that it 'might come in handy for the holocaust'. By an unspoken agreement they had told no one of their crazy derelict purchase, not even the children themselves, and when they had visited it last year (leaving Phip and Marion with her parents), they had stocked the farmhouse with candles and tinned food, coal, and medicines, like squirrels sensing a bad winter. And now if she had read the signs right, their caution had been justified.

The first city guard post appeared in her headlights, and she stopped, pulling in politely to the barrier and offering her papers for scrutiny.

'I'm just taking the children on a camping holiday,' she explained, every breath swelling in her chest. 'We're going north to Scotland. Their grandparents live in Edinburgh.'

At every barrier she gave the same explanation while her papers were read, and turned over, and stamped, and taken inside for checking against the Immigrants' List. As each city street appeared she saw the usual boarded-up shops and barricaded garages and hoped fervently that her petrol quota would take her far enough. She had enough stamps from her monthly allowance for a further four gallons, providing she could find a garage willing to serve her.

As she'd anticipated, there was very little traffic on the motorway: a few goods lorries which had evaded the picket lines, their names painted out to avoid detection and reprisal, a convoy of army transporters and the occasional family car. Several bore cases on their roof-racks or towed caravans or trailers, and she wondered if they too had decided it was time to leave the cities. Otherwise, there was no evidence of the troubles, though the bulletins were becoming more significant by the hour.

Her eyes were itching with tiredness. She'd never driven so far on her own before and for safety's sake she must rest. Rather than risk the publicity of a service station she turned off the motorway to a village she and Frank had visited several times. A light shone behind the boards at Mrs Malcolm's cafe, and with relief Kate parked the car at the back and introduced herself through the security phone. Fortunately, Mrs Malcolm remembered her. Kate resisted the temptation to order a full meal but sat on her own enjoying the rare luxury of a bacon sandwich. The radio was on, of course, and Kate was disturbed to learn that a curfew had been declared and all travellers ordered to return home. She must take to the back roads, and if stopped give her mother-in-law's address. Snatching up her handbag. she ran back to the car.

And so, for darkened mile after darkened mile she drove on, losing her way in one village and being stopped by a police car in another. The children began to stir, their sleep obviously becoming more natural.

By the time she reached the track off the main road her neck and shoulders ached unbearably, and she skidded on to the heather edge several times. The radio had suddenly gone dead, whether from poor reception or more sinister reasons she couldn't tell, but she put off her headlights to avoid detection, reducing her speed to a crawling five miles an hour.

At the crest of the ridge she stopped, staring in panic at the track below her. Even in daylight she had been too nervous to attempt it and had insisted that Frank drove that last three miles, but now there was no point in being timid and female. Somehow the car and the children sleeping in it had to be got down that track and there was only her to do it.

Turning back to the car, she was puzzled to see a

glare on the horizon. It couldn't be any natural trick of the dawn, for it came from the south and increased and dimmed in an irregular pattern. Stupidly, the possibility of fire didn't occur to her for a few seconds, then she stared at the sky in silent horror. The glare was the oil refinery at the port of T------, a few miles distant.

Getting back into the car she began the descent in absolute blackness, apart from the pale grey tinge of dawn. She daredn't put on the headlights; the men who had burnt the refinery could have chosen any route to escape and while she was sure they wouldn't deliberately hurt a woman with young children, anyone with petrol in their tank and food in their house would be at risk. She couldn't share with others, however selfish that might seem. Her children would need everything she had stored for them. It was as if some natural protective instinct had emerged from under layers of civilisation, giving her more courage than any man, and far greater ruthlessness. She cared nothing for the rights and wrongs of strikers, law, order, state or even husband, so long as she could drive that last three miles.

Marion awoke as soon as the car stopped and stared around her, expecting a camp site. She had been to the farm only once and had been told it was owned by one of Granddad's friends, so she couldn't understand why they had come now.

'I decided to rest here for a bit,' Kate lied. 'Come and help me get the trailer off.'

Together they struggled with the coupling and pushed the trailer into the stables, then Kate drove the car straight into the barn. The last few yards of the track had been muddy, and she went back along the route with a tarpaulin, showing Marion how to hold one corner and trail it over the tyre marks. The girl was puzzled but Kate explained that it was a game and they didn't want to be followed. Then she went back to the stables to take the air rifle from the tent bag before carrying the sleeping Phip into the house. She didn't dare put the lights on as the generator made so much noise, and she slipped several times. Fortunately, Marion was too sleepy to question any more, and quickly settled on the bed beside her brother. Gently Kate placed a blanket over them.

As soon as she went downstairs exhaustion hit her, and she slumped into the chair. For about an hour she slept, until her subconscious remembered that she hadn't put the shutters over the windows and she stumbled about the rooms, checking bolts. The sky was a hostile grey now and the portable radio crackled when she put it on, as if transmission had been resumed, and she left it tuned to BBC. Then a sound did come from it and startled her, leaving her shaking with fear and tiredness.

It was a young man's voice, certainly not the usual BBC tones, and breathless with excitement.

'This is the Students' Co-operative of Inner London,' he announced, 'speaking to the workers of Great Britain. The Prime Minister has resigned!'

There was some shuffling in the background as the voice continued.

'Acting on your behalf, a council of co-operatives

has been set up and is even now considering what action should be taken against those who have oppressed us. To our friends still struggling in the provinces, we send greetings. Our victory is assured.'

Apparently, victory was not quite as assured as he hoped, for there was the sound of shooting in the distance, and after a few further platitudes, the transmitter was once again silent.

During the early hours of that morning Kate dozed with the air rifle on her lap, startled occasionally into consciousness by the crackling of the radio. At eleven o'clock another voice proclaimed that the extremists had been overcome and peace was being restored in all but a few northern towns, but as no further broadcasts were made, this seemed unlikely. The children came downstairs, refreshed from a complete night's sleep and she struggled to remain patient with their questioning. They wanted to know why they hadn't gone camping and why they couldn't light a fire and why she hadn't slept in bed like a proper person and being too intelligent for ridiculous excuses about playing games or wanting to save money, they wouldn't be quiet until they received an answer. She couldn't find words however, and when the radio blurted into life again, she let that do her explaining.

This time the speaker was older. "This is the Official voice of the opposition," it began.

"We appeal for calm. The Government has resigned but we must have your help if we are to form another. Violence will solve nothing."

It was a stirring speech, hinting at but not naming the dreadful events of the night, arousing enough fear to bring about a return to sanity, but not enough to cause panic. The children sat small and frightened, trying to understand all the grown-up talk of pledges and reform and economic forces. Kate was too weary to care about such things, her mind focusing only on the fact that she ought to try and find some breakfast. Several prominent figures were mentioned, and her attention wandered until she heard that political prisoners had been released and thought of Frank. She was just recalling his worried face, when she heard his voice coming incongruously from the radio.

'When I wrote my book "The End of Western Society?" ten years ago, I did not dream that what I was imagining would come true. I was simply making a prediction, based on the evidence of history and certain trends I saw in modern society. Naturally I was pleased when critics praised my analysis, but I wanted to be wrong. Now I fear I am being proved at least partially right. Over five hundred people died last night in Birmingham during violent demonstrations, and the situation has been worse in London. Looting and mugging are taking place in all our cities, the T---- refinery has been destroyed, as have two of our newest nuclear reactors. Fortunately, the reactors themselves were shut off in time, but there is still danger of radioactive leakage. Bombs have exploded in Manchester and Bristol, killing women and children. Unless we come to our senses and control the forces of extremism in our country, this will be only the beginning. All over the Continent similar events are taking place. We must give the lead to check the violent men among us.'

The flatness of his voice showed how tired he was, and she doubted whether his new friends would be pleased at the details he gave (though they obviously thought it best not to cut him off). At least he was alive. That was something. His worst predictions might not come true, because he himself might be able to change the future he had predicted.

Yawning, she went out to the stables and began to unpack the trailer. By one of those peculiar ironies of life poor frightened Frank looked like finding himself converted by history into a hero, if he could survive long enough. And yet she doubted if he could have driven that last few miles in the darkness, or even have made the decision to leave in time. He would have wanted to stay a few days longer, to make sure, to check that they had everything they might need. Well, she didn't begrudge him his heroism, or the cleverness of the other men; she was only an insignificant housewife who had left school at 16 and worked as a dull computer programmer. She didn't understand all their talk; talk had simply produced that glare on the horizon. She had the next generation in her charge, and all she desired was to be allowed to rear it in peace. For a while at least, her fear had secured that right.

Taking the camping stove and the tins of rifle pellets, she went inside to make a pot of tea.

Glebe House

The house was far too big for them and needed so much work that a less obstinate person would have given up, but Josie was determined. They could afford the risk. George's building firm was doing well, and there was her income as a district nurse too. Besides, she was the only one in the family who appreciated what Glebe House meant. To the rest, the story of Grandfather's bankruptcy was one of those boring tales told at Christmas parties. As long as Josie could remember, the house had fascinated her. It should be theirs still, cared for and loved, not divided into sordid little flats.

And so, despite the advice of friends, she persuaded George to buy the house, and they opened the door onto a year of chaos. At weekends George worked harder than he ever did for his clients, and even little Gary helped, pushing his plastic wheelbarrow full of pieces of brick. Anthony's interest was caught too. He had a fascination for anything old, fostered by his history teacher. It was Anthony who discovered the well in the garden, and the missing cold slab, filling a gap in the wall. With great ceremony, they helped him bring it back to its rightful place in the larder.

That afternoon, Josie began to hear her voices. She could distinguish no words, just a distant hum of conversation in the front lounge, but the sound annoyed her. However, since nobody else mentioned it, she decided she was suffering from high blood pressure, and vowed not to carry stone slabs too often.

For several weeks afterwards, Josie forgot about the incident, and concentrated on clearing the bedrooms and the attic. She was overdoing things again, though. The clinic was one nurse short and she was working more hours than usual. Her head hummed with tiredness. Pausing as she swept, Josie tried to picture the room as it had once been - a servant's quarters no doubt. "Poor skivvy", she thought, pitying a life of endless scrubbing.

Then the voice spoke. "I'm so tired," it said. In terror, Josie swung round, expecting to see a young girl, but there was no one. Nothing. Just an empty room with bare boards. She ran from the attic.

Later, she tried to reassure herself. The fear she had felt was irrational, the result of stress. She must take things more easily. It did not matter how long they took to finish the house, and it would do no good to have her health break down.

After that, progress slowed, but even so, Glebe House was returning to its old self. The Civic Society began to take notice and invited George to speak at one of their meetings - "as if he had done all the work", Josie thought in disgust. He came home convinced that the building was older than it appeared, the front having been restored during the nineteenth century. Josie was less surprised than he was. She had always believed their home was given to her ancestors by James the First.

Once again, it was Anthony who helped. He seemed to have a gift for seeing the old beneath the new and removed some of the Victorian plaster in the cellar. A low doorway was revealed, which led to a further cellar. This had been partially filled when the front of the house was re-built. Inside was an old sink and a cooking range. Anthony was so excited he set about tracing the history of Glebe House, and disappeared for hours, to search through parish registers in the public library.

The uncovering of the cellar disturbed a lot of dust. It disturbed other things too. From that day onwards, Josie was haunted by voices only she could hear. A woman shouted orders raucously near the range; a boy laughed in Gary's room, a baby cried in the attic. In the attic too she heard the young girl again, sighing in exhaustion. The most distressing of all the voices was that of a woman crying, inconsolably, throughout the front of the house, but particularly near the window in Anthony's room. Josie was reduced to making excuses about not wasting time cleaning there until Anthony cleared up his mess ...

In the end, she visited the doctor, but did not have the courage to explain to him what she was hearing. The decongestant he prescribed was useless. Finally, she collapsed in the bathroom. Influenza had waited until she had the time and inclination to be ill.

George was a poor nurse but meant well. Josie did try to tell him about her voices, but he replied that people often heard funny things when they had the flu, so she gave up, and went to sleep.

Just after nine o'clock Josie woke, unable to decide what had disturbed her. Then she heard it again. That awful crying. It was as if the woman had come into her room and stood beside her bed. Gradually the sounds shaped themselves into words. "How will they manage without me?"

Sitting up, Josie stared into the dark. She must see who spoke. Perhaps she finally dozed, for it seemed that a shape formed near her: a young woman in a brocaded dressing gown. "My children," she said. "What happened to them?"

Josie was no longer afraid. All fear had left her, lost in a sense of shared motherhood. "I don't know," she replied. "But tell me their names. I'll try to find out."

"Charlotte and Henry. Charlotte was so bonny, but Henry was always ailing. Even if he survived, he would never have stayed well without my love."

"Survived what?"

"The fire. I was always afraid of that cook -- but Martha left so suddenly, and we had to have someone. Did my children live?"

A memory of an old glass photograph returned to Josie. She tried to recall the face. Her Barnsley Grandmother had shown it to her once, saying that the stern gentleman with the scars on his hands was Granny's father, who had owned a mill. His name had been Henry.

"Yes," Josie said, stretching out her hand in comfort. "I think Henry did. He was my --" She paused, trying to work out the relationship. "My great grandfather. He had several children. There was another branch of the family too, so perhaps Charlotte survived as well."

"I've never known," the woman said. "And no one cared enough to tell me." Silently, she went through the door.

When she recovered, Josie smiled at her own foolishness. 'Flu could certainly play some funny tricks. Then Anthony came back from the library clutching a photocopied newspaper report. There had been a fire at Glebe House, over a century ago. Most of the front of the house had been gutted, including the room Josie and George now used. Apparently the cook employed then had been in the habit of helping herself to the sherry, and had fallen asleep in the lounge with a candle burning. She and her mistress had both died. Fortunately a servant girl had been unable to sleep, and had managed to get down the back stairs with the baby. She had saved the little boy too, though his hands were badly burnt. The children's father was away at the time.

Quietly, Josie asked if she could borrow the photocopy. She read it again in her bedroom. The year was 1848 ...

That night she woke in terror. She had a distinct memory of a woman sitting beside her, holding the cutting. The woman had been upset at the details it gave, but relieved to hear that her children were saved.

She would like to see the glass plate of Henry she said.

After that, Josie was obsessed by the photograph. Unable to explain to George, she could only plead that she was longing to see her relatives in Barnsley again. So, reluctantly, George and the children sat at Cousin Jan's one Sunday afternoon, while Josie talked family gossip. When she could at last bring herself to mention the photograph, her cousin remembered it at once. Going into her bedroom, she fetched an old, carved box from under the bed. Taking out the glass photograph and a purse wrapped in a length of lace, Jan offered them to Josie. They belonged to an ancestor she said, and Josie would appreciate them more.

Thanking her cousin, Josie opened the purse. A small miniature had been placed inside. In amazement, she looked at the face painted upon it. The woman who stared back at her was the woman who had cried beside her bed.

At ten past three that night Josie woke, cold with fear. "He grew to be a fine wealthy man," a voice said. "These are mine you know. I never did like the portrait. It made my face too round. There's a sovereign hidden in the lining of the purse. I kept it there in case I ever needed it. Give it to Anthony."

Though she stared and stared into the darkness, Josie could see no one.

All the next day, the voices were particularly troublesome. The crying had stopped but the harsh voice near the cellar range was louder than ever, and more unpleasant. It became so threatening Josie dared not go down, not even for fuel. When she went to bed that night she lay in fear, only falling asleep after George had insisted on a couple of aspirins.

She dreamt that she felt the touch of fingers on her face. "You must leave this house," the woman's voice said. "Wake your husband and children and leave at once."

Bewildered, Josie began to argue. "Just go!" the voice insisted. "Your kindness to me broke the pattern, but that woman is as bad in death, as in life. It'll take time for me to persuade her. You're not safe tonight."

George was understandably cross when Josie woke him. He told her in no uncertain terms to go back to sleep. Such was her evident terror however, that he agreed to take the children outside, though he promised her a cold night on the lawn if she was playing some sort of game. Without thinking, Josie snatched up the purse and wrapped the lace around it as she ran downstairs. Shivering in her dressing gown, she stood foolishly in the front garden trying to explain.

George was about to storm back indoors when a flickering redness appeared behind the curtains. For a few seconds he stood in horror watching it spread across the lounge, then he was banging on a neighbour's door and shouting for the fire brigade.

Glebe House was not too badly damaged - though had the alarm not been given so quickly the whole front would have been gutted. The fire had started in the lounge, apparently beside a small Victorian table, and had spread rapidly to the front stairs - towards the bedroom in which George and Josie had been sleeping. An electrical fault must have caused it. There was no other explanation.

When Anthony pointed out the similarity to the fire of 1848, George said little. He went very quiet, merely agreeing with the fire officer that they were lucky to be alive.

The next morning as they sat in the blackened kitchen, George rubbed his eyes with the palms of his hands. "We'll get the insurance claim sorted out," he said, "And the repairs done, then I think we should move. Two fires are enough."

"Not after so much work," Josie pleaded. "It'll be all right now. You'll see. I know it will be."

Idly she put her hand into her dressing gown pocket and felt the purse with its wrapping of lace. "I wonder why I grabbed these," she remarked. Taking out the miniature, she turned the purse in her hand. Something hard moved inside the lining. Opening a tear in the silk, she pushed the object through. It was a bright, golden sovereign.

The Tennis Girls

―――

He often sat in the park, especially when Wimbledon was on TV. It amused him to see how many people dug their racquets out of cupboards for a few weeks. He liked to watch the girls playing on the old courts and listen to the snippets of life passing his bench.

"Potatoes. And carrots. And what about spaghetti?"

And what about spaghetti indeed? Sam smiled at the memory. Momma da Mario had ladled the stuff into them. They didn't dare complain. With her arms folded across her bosoms she looked like a sergeant major. She must have had a spaghetti tree in the garden. Still, he remembered holidays at her farm with fondness, and he couldn't afford much better in those days, not on Army pay. They were good days though, spending his leave with Polly, away from his mother.

"So, I says to him," a voice said near his bench, "'You need one of them deodorant sprays. That'll dry you out. I can't bear to wash your shirts.'"

"Missing girl found dead on Common" a car radio blared. One of the women glanced towards the car park.

"They've found that poor girl," she said. "Terrible. So young too."

Her companion wasn't listening, still too busy with her own topic. "George really is the limit. I told him I was going to send the invitations, but he has to send them. Now everyone will have two."

George? Who was George? The name rang a bell from his Gulf War days. Ah yes, he was the Geordie lad, the one who used to mimic the Sergeant behind his back. Fell in the latrine… They had the emptiest mess hut in Iraq. Even the hawkers stayed away that day.

"Sorry," a girl called across the court. "I keep forgetting we're not playing doubles."

Her companion laughed. "My game!" she announced.

Cricket was his game at school. He used to look good in white flannels. Smiling again, he recalled that last cup match against St. Bart's. Eighty-six in the shade. There he was, sweat pouring off his face and the Umpire looking at his watch. A six! A beautiful six! They carried him to the pavilion on their shoulders.

The tennis girls were giggling. "Look at Mr Rowlings," the blond one whispered, audible through the wire netting. He realised he'd been enacting the game with his hands and sat very still. Let them laugh. They never saw such a game.

The girls lounged against the net. "I can't stand these shorts," the dark one complained. "Mum says they go with my red top, but I hate that too."

He had hated the tennis club blazer and panama his

mother bought him. "Turn right round," she'd instructed. "Isn't he smart?" But his father had laughed. "Looks like he's on the stage," he joked. "Do us a dance, Sammy." When was that? He could only have been about nine or ten...

A ball rolled at his feet, startling him. "Chuck us our ball, Mister Rowlings," a voice called. Picking up the ball, he threw it, way beyond the children. "Oi Mister," the boy called again. "You didn't have to throw so hard."

Satisfied, Sam Rowlings settled back on his bench. He could show them a thing or two, for all he was nearly sixty. All those evenings in the camp gymnasium had paid off. In his prime he could lift eighty pounds. The lads who used to push him around in the Mess treated him with respect then. And the girls; it was amazing how they suddenly started talking to him.

A plump woman was struggling across the gravel, pushing a pram and hauling a weary toddler. She saw the space beside him. "This anyone's seat?" she asked and without waiting for a reply flopped on the bench. "It's a warm un isn't it?" she added, loosening her cardigan. "Too warm to be dragging little ones, but their Mum's at work and I couldn't stand it inside a moment longer."

She was the sort who could tell her life story in five minutes. "If you ask me," she continued, "a mother's place is at home, but you know these young women. They must have their washers and freezers and holidays abroad. I've told her, 'You're lucky to have a Mum to mind them, my girl'." She sniffed fondly, then paused, staring at him. "It's Mr. Rowlings isn't it? Well, I never. I didn't recognise you. Been ill, have you? I was sorry to hear of your mother's death. Still, she had a good innings. You remember me surely? Madge Hutchinson. We moved away a few years ago. I came back when my Bill died. I remember your mother well. A fine figure of a woman. She always had a sharp tongue, but she did a lot of good for the town…"

He grunted in the right places, not minding a bit of company. The days were long, even with the tennis girls to watch. Mrs. Hutchinson nodded in sympathy. "Your mother used to play a lot of tennis, didn't she?" she asked. "I remember now. She played for the County when I was a girl." Then she smiled, the sort of smile that says, 'Of course, my dear, I understand.'

"I expect you like to come here and think of her. I used to go to all Bill's haunts after he died."

The car radio was quieter now, as if the driver had wound the window up, but it was still audible. The news reader had finished the headlines and was giving details. "The body is thought to be that of Janine Fleming…"

"They've found that girl you know," Mrs. Hutchinson interrupted. "They say her attacker must have followed her onto the Common. The Police found her tennis racquet first."

She shuddered in horrified delight. "And no one noticed a soul, no one suspicious looking, not even a stranger. Just think, the murderer could have been sitting on this very bench." She nudged him to emphasise her point. "The Police were searching all round the park this morning you know, and yesterday. I watched them from my window."

He had seen them himself. Two constables and a man from C.I.D..

"Fifteen Love" one of the tennis girls called.

Sam Rowlings watched with pleasure. It was good to see young people like her, with their bright faces and lithe movements. He remembered how his Polly used to look in the firelight. Those girls playing tennis were thin compared to her. Why did the young women diet nowadays? A man liked something to get hold of. Polly was always so comfortable. If she had married him things would have been different, but his mother's constant interfering scared her off, just as it had scared off every other girl before then and since…

Sighing, he returned to the present. The tennis girls were laughing, their voices like bells out of tune. The blond one reminded him of a photograph of his mother that used to stand on the mantlepiece. She was lithe and pretty before she married his father, though her expression even then was sour…

Madge Hutchinson was leaving, pushing her pram through the gates and down the road. He turned back to the game in front of him. Yes, the blond looked like his mother. Even her hair was the same and the bright red lipstick.

Taking out his sandwiches, he began to eat, slowly and methodically. All the while, he watched the tennis girls playing in front of him. He was still watching when they picked up their racquets and collected their balls. They slammed the iron gate, making little flecks of rust fly in his face.

"What are you staring at?" the blond one asked him rudely. "Haven't you got something better to do?" She definitely reminded him of his mother.

He wished she didn't. It was cruel of her, almost as cruel as his mother had been. Not that others would have thought his mother cruel. To them she was Jean Rowlings, the celebrated tennis player, organiser of raffles, opener of bazaars, manager of committees. But a child sees the private side. If she had let him become a person instead of treating him like one of her possessions, he could have forgiven her, but he'd had to get away. Joining the Army was his only route. It was her fault he had almost died, her fault that he'd seen his best mate blown to pieces beside him…

"Perhaps he likes your legs," the dark one suggested, "Dirty old man!" the blond replied.

Both tennis girls shrieked with laughter.

They walked towards the fork in the path, where they stood chatting and giggling for another ten minutes. Finally, they parted, the dark one into the street, the blond taking the route towards the Common. "See you tomorrow," she called to her friend. Then she set off, swinging her racquet.

Quietly Sam got up and followed her.

He wasn't nervous. An icy calmness had begun to fill his mind. He'd get away with it again. He always did. The police hadn't even questioned him. No one ever noticed him.

Suddenly the girl turned back, almost bumping into him. "Mel!" she called. "I forgot to give you your invitation." Running past him, she disappeared towards the road.

Bandstand

"So, tell me what happened."

"Ok...........but where d'yer want me to start?"

"How about starting at the beginning?"

"I dunno where the beginning is, to be honest, mate."

"Well, why don't you start where you think the beginning is?"

"Ok, how about them missing tennis balls."

"Fine, let's start there then."

…

Rose was watching the bush with amusement. She couldn't see Alan at all. Rather, all she could see was a large shrub, quivering like a giant insect. The bush was swearing too.

"Alan, I've got another ball. It doesn't matter!" she called out to the bush.

With a loud "humph" Alan reappeared. "I know the ball went into that bush," he shouted back. "But I'm damned if I can find where it went." He walked back to the tennis court, morosely. "That's the fifth ball we've lost this week."

"Yes, alright, I know," Rose replied. It probably was her fault each time the ball had gone sailing out of the court. It was just that she didn't have as much control of her forehand as she'd had before. What she'd lost in control or accuracy, however, she hadn't lost in power. It had been a superb shot, or it would have been if she hadn't sent the ball into mini orbit, straight into the nearby foliage. She used to beat Alan regularly, but now their games were much more even. That was one thing about retirement, she thought to herself. You have more time to do the things you enjoy, but you're not as good at them as you used to be.

Reaching into her bag, she retrieved another tennis ball. She noted with some annoyance that it was their last. She concentrated hard on making sure her service was in. It was much slower as a result, and Alan returned it with ease.

It didn't take that long for the inevitable to occur. It was again a lapse of concentration on her part. A rather over ambitious shot sailed over Alan's head into the undergrowth. She watched it closely, making sure she noted where it landed. Beating Alan out of the court, she ran towards the ball's landing site. She was certain of success; the ball had fallen right in front of a rather unusual pale green plant with white flowers. Surely, she couldn't fail to find it?

She stood in front of the plant, mystified. She was sure her eyes could make out a little dimple in the soil, where the ball had landed. Of the ball itself, there was absolutely no trace. She looked around to see if it could have rolled anywhere. It didn't seem likely, as the ground was flat. Turning, she saw one of the park-keepers painstakingly weeding a border of flowers. She jogged a few steps towards him.

"Excuse me," Rose tried her most charming smile. "But you haven't seen a tennis ball by any chance?"

She was surprised. The gardener ignored her completely. He didn't even look up. She watched him carry on his weeding. Something stopped her speaking to him again. Maybe it was his extreme concentration on the weeds in front of him. Maybe it was the way he had turned his back as she'd approached. She couldn't see his face clearly; he'd pulled his woollen hat low over his brow.

Puzzled, she glanced back at Alan and shrugged. She walked back towards the court, trying to find something to say. It was nearly lunchtime so perhaps it was no bad thing they couldn't carry on. Still, she just couldn't understand why they kept losing their tennis balls. It never occurred to her to have a look in the gardener's basket. All she could see was a mass of dead weeds. If she had looked beneath that cover, however, she'd have had another surprise. She'd have found her missing tennis balls, not just from today, but from earlier in the week too.

...

"Well, I suppose taking tennis balls is theft, but it hardly means the gardener is the devil incarnate," the Vicar commented.

"Hey, you said start at the beginning. It gets worser," was the reply.

"In what way? Did he start taking tennis balls while people were still holding them? I could call the police and report him for assault."

"He's done much more than that, mate."

"Give me another example then."

"Alright, he follows people with dogs around. You know, to see if they clean up after their pooches."

...

It was a cool November morning. The ground and air were damp. Leaves glistened in the pale sunshine. A multitude of cobwebs sparkled like jewels along the hedges of dark green holly. Claire was aware that she could see her breath, like wisps of smoke rising to the skies. She tightened her grip on Milo's lead. He looked up at her briefly, but swiftly went back to the far more important business of sniffing every millimetre of the park.

As they turned the corner towards the ornamental pond, Claire became aware of a presence. Rather, she felt that she was being watched. She didn't turn immediately. She'd had that feeling before in the park, whenever she was with Milo. She felt safe, thankfully. Although Milo was a gentle dog, he was also a huge German

Shepherd. Not many people would try to harm her when he was around. She joked that he was probably bigger than the Hound of the Baskervilles. He scared people without meaning to. It was probably a constant source of bewilderment to Milo. He never seemed to understand why people shied away from him when all he wanted was to say hello. Anyone with enough courage to fuss Milo soon found he was quite happy to stand for hours on end having his head stroked. Fortunately for Claire, not many people ever made that discovery.

She allowed herself a little glance to her left, as Milo snuffled through some fallen leaves. He seemed to love autumn in particular. She'd noticed before how he'd make a point of walking under trees, just to hear the sound of the leaves under his large feet.

At first, she couldn't see anyone. Then her eyes became more accustomed to the slight gloom between the trees. She could see the older gardener, the one with absolutely no hair. Usually, he wore a woolly hat when he was gardening, but today his head was bare. For some reason, it gave her a start. She wasn't sure why at first. It was quite normal for the gardener to be standing in his park. That was his job, after all. Except, Claire reflected, that his job was to weed and plant things, not to stand silently, watching people.

Claire decided to move on, tugging an indignant Milo with her. She wanted to put some distance between them and Mr Spooky-no-hair. They walked away briskly, Claire tugging at Milo's lead whenever she felt him slow down. After a few minutes, she risked looking back again. She noted with a start that the gardener was almost exactly the same distance away as before. He must have kept up with them deliberately. Claire was starting to get alarmed now. She could see absolutely no reason why the gardener would be following them. After all, it was a popular place to take a dog and, as required, she never let Milo off his lead.

She pulled Milo along again, this time tugging so hard he yelped with displeasure. She reached down to fondle his ear, as an apology, but kept him moving quickly along. She knew he would much rather spend half an hour sniffing one interesting blade of grass, than speed-walk around the park. Still, in the circumstances, she felt that her needs were greater than his.

Glancing over her shoulder, she could see movement from the corner of her eye. Stopping, she turned to stare. The gardener was almost jogging to keep up with them. Claire thought frantically. Whilst Milo could easily outrun their pursuer, he could also outrun Claire. She made a snap decision. Wheeling round to face the way they'd come, Claire tugged an astonished Milo in her wake. She was now almost running towards the gardener. If she couldn't get away from him, she figured, she'd see what he did when she went towards him.

She was closing the gap between them, rapidly, Milo bouncing along beside her. She was watching the gardener to see what he'd do. He came to an abrupt halt, glanced quickly to either side of him, and then disappeared to his right.

Claire and Milo didn't take long to get to the spot

where the bald gardener had paused. To Claire's amazement, there was absolutely no trace of him. She decided against searching the undergrowth. She felt that she'd made her point. Shaking slightly, she took Milo towards the exit at a more leisurely but still brisk pace. She wasn't sure she'd walk in the park again, not without her husband anyway.

As they left the park, Claire realised with a start that the gardener was just to her right. He must have run to get ahead of them. Feeling her skin go cold, she turned to look at him. He was standing in front of the holly hedge that ran along the pathway. Despite herself, she was curious and stopped to get a better look at what he was doing. He seemed to be wiping the hedge. She strained her eyes to see more clearly. As he moved closer, she saw. He was plucking cobwebs out of the hedge. Pulling Milo, Claire ran all the way home.

…

"Oh dear," the Vicar poured another cup of tea for his visitor. "I can see how the young lady would be quite alarmed. Do you know whether she reported it to the police?"

"Nope she didn't. The others didn't, neither. She weren't the only one he spooked out like that." The visitor added three cubes of sugar to his fresh tea.

"Well, I'm not sure there's much I can do unless someone actually makes a complaint. I suppose I could warn my parishioners to watch out for him, so they're not alarmed. I know quite a few of my "flock" walk their dogs in the park."

"You should warn 'em not to drop litter, neither. He made some punk kids pick up all the stuff they'd dropped."

"Well there's nothing wrong with that. I do the same; I always make children put their litter in the bin."

"Ah, but I bet you don't have a gun!"

...

Mr Reynolds passed a hand through his hair. He was definitely getting a little greyer now. Still, everyone said how distinguished it made him look. He was glad to look a tad older, to be honest. He'd already noted how it made the parents treat him with a bit more respect.

Sighing, he collected the books on his desk into a semi-neat pile, tidy enough to fit into his shoulder bag. He hadn't had a good day, but he knew not to be disheartened. There would be good days ahead, and sadly bad ones too. The knack was not to dwell on the bad days. He also knew that it was partly due to exhaustion. It was a long term, fortunately with the holidays just a few weeks away. Then he'd be able to re-charge his batteries, as his partner called it, fresh for the new term.

Part of the problem was his year ten class. He knew that it was hard for the kids these days, with all the exams, league results tables and parental pressure. The latter would be much worse, he thought, at the private school he'd turned down all those years ago. Then he'd been full of optimism about working for a state school; all that enthusiasm for making sure the "free" education was of the highest standard. He still agreed with the choice he'd made, even if days like today made it that much harder to carry on.

The main problem was Luke. There was no doubting that Luke was 'leader of the pack'. Whatever Luke did, you could guarantee at least three or four of the quieter kids would follow suit. Luke was involved in every bit of 'bother', every noisy disruption. It might of course be boredom. Mr Reynolds recognised that Luke was bright. Indeed, that was how Luke had managed to scrape through so far with minimal effort and almost zero concentration. Mr Reynolds had seen it all before, sadly. It was nearly always in year ten that boys like Luke 'came a cropper'. Suddenly it was serious; there were exams to pass, coursework to complete and hand in on time. Even if Luke did manage to pass this year, the same probably wouldn't be true for a number of the boys riding in his wake.

The even bigger problem, Mr Reynolds realised, was that Luke was funny. It was often hard to keep a straight face when Luke was doing one of his 'turns'. Today, it had been a reasonably accurate impression of the headmaster. Yesterday's was a hilarious rendition of the school song, backwards. It was hard to keep control of a class when the teacher himself was close to having a fit of giggles. It also made it harder to discipline Luke properly.

Mr Reynolds turned with a sigh to the door of his classroom. He was just about to leave when Danny ran in, knocking the door violently towards Mr Reynolds.

"Steady, boy!" Mr Reynolds admonished. "It's not normal for you to be in such a hurry to come into the classroom. Usually, you can't get out quick enough!"

Danny was momentarily speechless. Mr Reynolds realised it wasn't his stunning wit that kept the child silent. Danny was breathing so hard, he was in danger of hyperventilating.

"Slow down, Danny, or you'll do yourself an injury. Here, sit on this chair and tell me what the rush is all about." Mr Reynolds slid one of the chairs over towards the region of Danny's rear end. When the boy didn't move, Mr Reynolds found that a gentle shove had the desired effect.

Once seated, Danny's breathing became more regular. Mr Reynolds himself breathed a sigh of relief. He'd been wondering if he'd need to call an ambulance.

"It's Luke," Danny finally managed to gasp out.

"What's he done now?" Mr Reynolds grimaced.

"He dropped some litter and there's this old geezer with no hair. He's got a gun to Luke's head!"

Mr Reynolds eyed Danny carefully. In his youth, Mr Reynolds would have sounded the immediate alarm, calling a police armed response unit to rescue Luke. Nowadays, Mr Reynolds was more cautious. He'd been caught out before by tall stories told by children with overactive imaginations.

"Where are this 'old geezer' and Luke?" Mr Reynolds asked, calmly.

"Down in the park. We was all walking through on

our ways home, like."

"I see your grammar still needs some work, Danny. Why don't you show me the way and I'll take a look for myself."

Danny looked reluctant to move. Mr Reynolds realised this could be for one of two reasons. Either Danny was scared to go back because there really was someone holding Luke at gun point. Or Danny knew he'd be shown up for telling lies. Mr Reynolds preferred the second explanation.

Scraping the chair back, Danny shrugged and led the way out of the classroom. Mr Reynolds followed him through the playground, to the school gate near the park. Entering the park, Danny led the way towards the bandstand.

The route really didn't surprise Mr Reynolds. He'd long known that the bandstand was an out of hours meeting place, often involving under-age drinking, or smoking, or both. The 'evidence' was usually there for all to see the next day. Mr Reynolds presumed that today one of the park gardeners had caught Luke in action. Perhaps the 'old geezer' really had flipped.

The sight that met Mr Reynolds' eyes was one he'd find hard to forget. Luke was with two smaller boys, probably from year seven. They were all three on hands and feet, crawling around the base of the bandstand. At first, Mr Reynolds thought the boys were crouching down to be sick. He then saw that they were picking up cigarette buts and small bits of broken glass from the lawn around the bandstand. They were each carrying a small plastic carrier bag to put the litter into. Judging by the amount they'd picked up, they'd been doing their impromptu rubbish collection service for some time.

The explanation for their good deed of the day stood slightly to one side. He was indeed an 'old geezer' in teenage boy terms. Mr Reynolds judged the gardener to be in his late fifties, possibly older. He might well be bald, but for the time being his head was covered with a blue woolly hat. He was glaring at the three boys, arms folded in front of him. The whole scene felt slightly surreal.

With a start, Mr Reynolds noticed the gun. He should have realised that Luke would never voluntarily clean up anything without an extremely good inducement. Moving forwards, Mr Reynolds coughed nervously. "Erm, excuse me," he said as he approached the gardener. There was absolutely no response.

"I think you're quite right to make the boys clear up," Mr Reynolds tried again. "But do you really think aiming a gun at them is the right idea?" He moved further forwards cautiously.

Again, his words produced no reaction. Mr Reynolds stopped and considered the gun. He didn't know much about firearms, but this one looked like something you'd find in a museum, possibly from the 'Great War'. Looking at the implacable gardener, Mr Reynolds could picture him occupying a trench at Ypres.

Mr Reynolds took stock of the situation. He was getting nowhere talking to the gardener. Maybe he could try to get the boys to walk away slowly, once they'd picked up all the litter of course. He turned to look at the quivering Danny near the hedge, his white face gleaming like a waning moon. The crawling boys in front of him were in the most danger, being the closer targets. Perhaps he could get them to crawl to the other side of the bandstand. At least that would give them some cover if the gardener did open fire. Mr Reynolds looked back at the gardener, to judge whether he would actually use the gun.

But the gardener was no longer there.

A rapid glance around showed he was nowhere to be seen. "Did you see which way he went?" Mr Reynolds called over to the quivering Danny.

"He just disappeared," was the shaky reply.

"I can see that, but which way did he disappear?"

"He didn't go any way. He just disappeared!" Danny was starting to sob. The other boys had risen to their feet, cautiously glancing around them to see if the coast really was clear.

It was, of course, Luke who acted first. Dropping his carrier bag of rubbish, he scarpered, followed shortly by the two smaller lads. Danny recovered enough to find his legs and made a hasty exit back towards the school.

Mr Reynolds was left alone, with three plastic carrier bags full of rubbish, an empty bandstand and a huge uncertainty as to what had just happened. He was certain of only one fact: that the ground around the bandstand was cleaner than it had been for years.

…

"Goodness me!" exclaimed the Vicar. "We really do need to report your colleague. He can't go around brandishing guns at children: even if they were litter louts!"

"Hey, that weirdo ain't no colleague of mine," the visitor retorted.

"But I thought you work down at the park as one of the gardeners. I presumed this gardener was one of your colleagues." The Vicar was puzzled.

"Oh well, yeah I'm one of the gardeners alright."

"Good, well tell me the name of this other gardener so I can report him to the police. I'll do it myself today."

"Won't do you no good. That's why I come to you, not the coppers, innit."

"Excuse me?"

"The other geezer – he's dead."

"Oh, I see" although the Vicar felt that really he didn't. "What did he die of?"

"I dunno. His 'eart or something."

"Well I guess that's probably to be expected. He seems to have been a very angry man. Stalking young women, holding children hostage at gun point. It doesn't surprise me he's driven himself to a heart attack."

"You don't get it do yer? His name was William Carter, gardener for the big house. Police can't help us. Bill Carter died in 1929. Now do you get why I came to see yer? You God-types can do exorcisms, right?"

The Rains

REG WAS WASHING HIS NEW CAR; AGAIN. IT WAS THE second time this week. Not that the car was dirty, Ian thought. After all, it was less than a month old and had hardly been used. Still, if Ian had a brand-new red sports car, he'd probably be out cleaning it every day too. He glanced at his ancient Volvo in the drive and shrugged. Turning, he saw his daughter doing her school homework at the kitchen table and remembered why he couldn't afford a new sports car. He would rather pay for her schooling.

"Hey, Dad," Gabrielle called, "come and look at this."

Ian left the window and crossed to his daughter. He was immensely proud of Gabrielle. Like her sadly deceased mother, she was thin and elegant with jet black hair. At 14 she was just starting to turn from girl to young woman. Ian knew it wouldn't be long before she started taking an interest in boys. The boys had been taking an interest in her for a couple of years. Fortunately, she'd also inherited her father's love of books and, so far, hadn't noticed.

"What am I meant to be looking at?" he asked.

"This bit on ancient fairy tales and myths. We've been asked to find old stories that can still be relevant today, for a project. I've just been reading about the legend of St. Swithin. Did you know that if it rains on St. Swithin's Day, it will rain for forty days and forty nights?"

"So I've heard. When is St. Swithin's Day?"

"Today."

Ian put his hand on his daughter's head. "Let's hope it doesn't rain," he teased. "Fortunately, we're forecast fine weather for the next three days. I'm afraid you're out of luck."

...

Dominic was poking the ground with a stick. "What are you doing?" his mother asked.

"Play ants" he replied.

They were sitting in the shelter of the cricket pavilion. Julia leaned over to see what Dominic was looking at. She immediately recoiled. She hadn't expected to see so many ants.

"Darling, I don't think you should poke the ants with a stick" she said and removed the stick from her son's hand. "You don't want to make them angry. Look! Some of them have wings, so they could fly at you if you poke them too hard".

Dominic looked upset at the loss of his stick. Julia quickly replaced it with a small slice of pork pie. Her son brightened and started munching.

Julia looked back at the ants. They were marching purposefully in a line across the terrace, towards the trees behind the pavilion. As she looked closer, she could see that some of them were carrying small white balls on their backs. She wondered if those were ant eggs and, if so, why the whole colony of ants was moving towards the trees.

She read the ledger again and sighed. It didn't matter how many times she checked; the numbers stayed the same. Putting the ledger back in her bag she looked around. The old club hut wasn't bad, but it could definitely do with a lick of paint and some new furniture. There was no hope of either, given the club's finances. She wasn't sure why she'd let herself be persuaded (or was it bullied?) into being the club's Treasurer.

Sighing, Julia glanced at the trees. All was quiet. She wondered why she couldn't hear the usual babble of birds. The sky was darkening, clouds mounding like grey candyfloss. After a month of dry sunny weather there was a chill in the air. It was quite a shock; it didn't feel like July at all. "Come along darling," she said to Dominic. "We'd better head home. Race you to the corner." Pretending to run, she hurried along the path towards the road, little Dominic trotting alongside her.

As they rounded the corner of the cricket field, a sudden wind blew. Startled, a squadron of angry crows rose into the sky, screeching. Julia watched as they circled over her. For some reason, she shuddered. "It looks like rain," she said over brightly, "and I haven't brought an umbrella. What a silly Mummy!"

Picking her son up, she quickened her pace.

...

Reg was gently stroking his new pride and joy. Who cared if the wife had wanted to go on a cruise? It was his pension lump sum, not hers, after all. And he'd always, always wanted a new sports car. A convertible of course, but not a soft top. He didn't trust them; thought they'd probably leak in the rain. So, he'd treated himself to a model which converted at the flick of a switch. He still loved watching the top go in and out of its little hidey-hole at the back.

Now all he needed was some nice weather to go zooming around in. He couldn't wait to see the neighbours' faces; they'd be so jealous. He'd seen Ian staring from his front window on the other side of the road. Well, let him ogle, Reg smiled to himself.

He glanced at the sky. A large cloud was forming. It looked like a hammer head. That often meant thunder, he recalled. He considered putting the new love of his life into the garage, but the lawn mower was still in bits on the floor. He'd have to get round to mending that first, and he'd far rather polish the car. Besides, rain wasn't forecast until Tuesday. The weatherman on TV had joked about missing St Swithin's Day.

...

"It looks like we may be safe after all." Ian remarked after lunch.

"What do you mean, Dad?" Gabrielle looked up, surprised.

"The sky's a little lighter. We'll be spared your forty days and nights of rain."

"Good, except that if it doesn't rain, I won't be able to prove whether the myth is true," Gabrielle replied, smiling. "I was hoping it would rain a bit, but then be sunny and warm for the rest of the summer, just to show the whole St Swithin thing is rubbish."

"I'm with you in wanting a nice summer." Ian agreed. "By the way, have you seen the ant powder? There's a lot of ants coming into the lounge from behind the skirting board."

"I think it's in the shed." Gabrielle looked up. "You'll also need some in the kitchen and the hallway. I saw some ants there earlier. They seemed to be intent on going up the walls. I have no idea why."

"Maybe they know better than the forecasters," Ian suggested, "and they're going for higher ground. Maybe you'll be able to test St. Swithin after all."

He was smiling as he went out to the shed.

...

"You know, I think St Swithin may have had a point," Gabrielle exclaimed. She was standing at the kitchen window later that afternoon, watching the sky. Rather than going away as her father had hoped, the clouds had thickened. The room was going dark, though it was only four o'clock. "If it does rain it'll be heavy." She glanced over her shoulder at her father.

"I hope we don't get forty days and nights of it, or there'll be floods," Ian replied, only half joking. "It's a good job we're not on the other side of the road. They always get loads of water in their drives when it rains heavily." He tried not to sound anxious. "Do you remember where I put that ant powder by the way?"

"What?" Gabrielle was surprised, not with her father losing the powder (that was par for the course) but that he needed it again. She left her vigil at the kitchen window and followed him into the hall. Then she stopped in astonishment. Each corner was black. It was too dark to see why, so she put the light on. At once a flurry of ants scurried back under the skirting boards. Others headed for the gap in the floorboards near the stairs.

"We don't have that much powder," Gabrielle said in alarm. "I've never seen so many ants." Recalling her biology classes, she tried to remember if there was anything else they could use. Perhaps if they looked at the ingredients on the box, they might be able to make something themselves. "Why have they come in?" she asked.

"I've no idea, but they seem to be going upwards," her father replied. "Maybe they're expecting a storm and are trying to stay dry."

"Shall we leave them to it, or kill them?" Gabrielle

asked. "It seems unfair to wipe them out, but I don't want ants in my bed." She grimaced at the thought. "But if they keep moving upwards, they'll end up in the attic, which is probably ok. I don't see they can do any damage there. Can we just leave them?"

"We may not have much choice," her father decided. "We don't have enough powder to keep them at bay forever. I don't think these are stinging ants, although I don't like the look of the ones with wings. If they just keep to the corners, we can step round them. It's not ideal, but I don't know what else to suggest. We could try putting sticky tape around things we don't want them on."

"I think you'd have to keep replacing the sticky tape," Gabrielle warned. "When the tape's full of dead ants, the others can just climb over them."

"What a horrible thought!" Ian replied, just as the telephone rang.

Gabrielle answered. "It's Julia from next door, Dad," she whispered. "She's really worried because they have ants everywhere and her little boy keeps playing with them. She doesn't know what to do. What shall I say?"

"Tell her she's welcome here, but we're in the same position. Though thankfully you're too old to play with ants these days."

Gabrielle snorted and turned back to the telephone.

"That's decided then," she announced as she put the phone down. "Julia and Dominic are coming round. She's going to bring any ant powder she can find. I'll make up the spare bed in the guest room for her, and she can put Dominic on the little sofa beside her."

His daughter's quiet efficiency impressed Ian. He wondered whether she was trying to match-make. Certainly, Julia was attractive, although about 10 years younger than him. More importantly she was divorced and, according to Gabrielle, this made her "available" for a lonely widower. Smiling, he stepped over a column of ants and ruffled his daughter's hair.

An hour later, Dominic was playing happily in the middle of the lounge. Gabrielle had found a box of toys from the recesses of her cupboard, annoying a hundred or so ants in the process. Julia had been in such a state that she'd arrived with nothing other than her son in her arms and two puffers of ant powder.

"I hate ants," Julia sighed. "Especially the ones with wings! They're absolutely everywhere in my house."

"As you can see," Ian replied, "we've got quite a few of our own. It's ok though," he added, seeing her concern, "they keep to the corners of the rooms, mainly on the skirting boards. We're leaving them alone and they're returning the compliment."

Gabrielle appeared, carrying a large sports bag filled with whatever she'd thought Julia and Dominic would need. She glanced quizzically at her father.

"I bet she's trying to work out how well I'm getting on with Julia," Ian thought.

...

Reg was incandescent with rage. He'd spent an hour

reassembling the lawn mower so he could put his pride and joy into the garage. But when he'd got into the car, the engine wouldn't start. He couldn't believe it. A brand-new sports car which goes from 0-60 in less than five seconds, and there it was, sitting on his drive unable to go anywhere. So, he'd run back into the house to get his wife to help push the car into the garage. Only she'd refused. She'd also suggested it might just need a good wash. It must be at least a couple of hours since he last did it. He was not impressed with her attitude.

Contemplating his next move Reg stood at the front door. He'd seen a number of people come and go at Ian's over the road. Maybe they'd help him push his car into the garage? He decided it was worth trying, and ran across the road, not stopping to tell his wife.

He arrived panting on Ian's doorstep. It was Gabrielle who opened the porch door. She looked surprised but let him into the hallway. "Hey Dad," she called out, "it's Mr Dutton from over the road."

"Come on in," she said to Reg,

Ian appeared in the hallway with Julia behind him. "We're having an impromptu house-party," he said drily. "You're welcome to join us."

Reg didn't stop to ask why Ian had his pretty neighbour at his house; he figured that she and Ian were healthy and strong enough to help push his car. He was about to ask for their assistance when he heard Gabrielle gasp. She'd closed the porch, but the front door was open. Her hand still on the doorknob, she was looking towards Reg's house. "That's strange," she said.

"What is, honey?" her father asked.

"I thought Mr Dutton's new car was red, but it's got black patches on it now."

Reg turned with astonishment. It was true. His car was black on the bonnet and doors, rather than the beautiful fire red that he'd paid for. There was no way anyone could have swapped the car when he wasn't looking, was there? He could feel anger brewing up inside him. Maybe his wife was playing a trick on him? Or someone had splashed paint on it?

"Hang on," Ian said. He reached for a pair of binoculars from the top drawer of the hall cupboard. He was focussing on the car when Reg pulled the binoculars out of his hand. Surprised, Ian protested but Reg didn't reply.

It was hard to see through the porch glass, but it looked to Reg as if his car was quivering. Bewildered, he handed the binoculars back to Ian. "Take a look," he said. Ian took them with a wry smile: he'd been trying to look when Reg snatched the binoculars from him. His smile faded. "That's odd" he said. "Your car definitely has black patches on it."

"I can see that," Reg snapped back. "What I can't see is why."

Ian shrugged and passed the binoculars to his daughter. She had better eyesight than he did. Gabrielle re-focussed the lenses and stared intently across the road.

"Oh…" she said softly and put her hand to her mouth. Ian turned to her in concern. "The car's covered in ants, Dad," she whispered. "That's why it's got black patches. They seem to be trying to climb onto the hood and slipping. Maybe they do know something we don't. I think we should move everything valuable upstairs…"

She realised Reg had heard. "I'm sure everything will be ok, Mr Dutton," she added quickly.

Reg pushed past them both. It was alright for her to say everything would be ok; she hadn't just spent over a hundred grand on a new car. He wasn't going to have it covered in ants. Goodness only knew what they'd do to it. They were probably already in the engine, which was why it wouldn't start.

He ran over the road towards his house, oblivious to everything but the car on his drive. He was scarcely aware of the squeal of brakes as a van swerved to avoid him. He dimly heard Gabrielle scream, but he was too intent on the black dots swarming over the bonnet to care. Grabbing a broom from the garage he started trying to brush them off. "Go away!" he shouted. "Get off!"

His wife appeared at a window. "We've got ants all over the house!" she shouted. "They're everywhere, even on the stairs. Leave that stupid car and do something!"

But Reg wasn't listening. He was staring at the thousands of ants crawling inside his new car.

Suddenly fat spots of water splashed onto his head.

It was beginning to rain…

We hope you enjoyed our short stories and maybe we can persuade you to try one of the DI Ambrose books, if you haven't already done so. Here's a 'taster' from Poetic Justice, the 4th DI Ambrose Mystery.

The DI Ambrose Mysteries can be read in any order and can be purchased from www.stairwellbooks.co.uk or from Amazon.

Poetic Justice

Friday 11th March 1960

Her pulse raced. Stopping quickly, Meadows turned to listen. She stared into the darkness behind her. There was no one in sight.

Catching her breath to steady it, she walked on. The footsteps began again. Once again Meadows stopped. So too did the steps.

In the silence she strained to hear movement. There was nothing except the wind in the overhead wires. Urgently she shone her torch around.

The alley took a wide sweep between the houses. It was impossible to see beyond the bend. A single street lamp lit a small circle of concrete but didn't reach the curve. She flashed her torch up and down the fences either side of the alley. There was nothing but wood, and a line of scrubby weeds.

Still WPC Meadows waited. If someone had been walking innocently behind her, they'd have caught up by now. No one appeared.

Finally, telling herself she was imagining things, she

continued her search. Her ears felt as if they were aching with the effort of listening: a train in the distance, a dog barking. Then she heard it again. Footsteps! But this time the walker was treading softly, almost inaudibly. She could be imagining the sound. Except that she knew she wasn't.

At once Meadows reached for her whistle. "Not that anyone's likely to come," she thought nervously. "Not round here." Still, the hard shape in her fingers made her feel better. "Pretend not to notice," she told herself. "Just keep going." She quickened her pace, but she didn't run. That might enrage a follower, who might well be quicker than her.

And when she came out of the alley, what then? Meadows tried to remember her training. "Find the nearest house with a light on, and bang on the door," she decided. "But supposing he catches up with me?" She couldn't recall anyone mentioning that bit. No one was likely to be up at this hour anyway.

"Hit him over the head with my handbag," Meadows thought wryly. Not for the first time she cursed being a woman. A male PC had a truncheon; a female officer was allowed a handbag and a whistle. "Fat lot of use!" she muttered to herself.

With every nerve stretched, Meadows walked out into the street, waiting for something to happen. But nothing did. The footsteps stopped. The night settled into early dawn. There was just the dog barking and the wind in the wires.

She let her breath out in relief. Perhaps the footsteps

had never existed. It was dark and cold and she was tired, after hours of looking for a couple of escapees from the local Approved School for Delinquent Boys. Maybe there was an echo in the passage. Or perhaps there really had been someone there, but they hadn't wanted to be seen by the police. She must check for reports of burglaries from the houses nearby.

The tower of St George's church loomed ahead and she walked briskly past the old graveyard. In the flickering light of a street lamp the church looked threatening and bleak. Pausing to listen again, Meadows shone her torch at the graveyard and across the car park, then went around the back to the hall and tried the door. It was locked, the wire screen over the window correctly in place.

Glad to move on, Meadows approached The Brigadier pub. That too was in darkness. As usual, she tried the main entrance, then checked the back. All the doors there were safely locked. Next she looked inside the bus shelter nearby. It would be a good hiding place for a couple of young desperados. Apart from some screwed up fish and chip papers, though, it was empty. They might have rested there earlier, but they were nowhere in sight now. Then she hurried towards the phone box at the end of St George's Avenue.

The box smelled of stale sweat as Meadows entered and she wrinkled her nose. Her hands were shaking as she fumbled with the coins, and she called herself an idiot for letting a trivial incident unnerve her. All the same, she would be glad to be back at the Police Station.

"Anything to report?" PC Higgins asked. "You're a bit late."

"Sorry, it was dark in the alleys." For a second Meadows paused, wondering whether to say more. She would sound a fool. No one had attacked her, or even made a threat. Reporting mysterious footsteps would only get her laughed at in the tearoom. "Meadows thinks she's got a follower!" the blokes would say. She could write the script.

"No, all quiet," she replied. "No sign of the runaways from Moorlands. I've been to all the usual places. I'm just off to check the shops on the High Street, in case they've bunked up there for the night. But it looks like they had their tea in the bus shelter, so I reckon they've left Chalk Heath by now. I'll be back in half an hour."

Opening the door of the phone box, she stared across the road.

A cloudy dawn was leaking over the rooftops. In the half-light something moved. A dark shape hurriedly stepped back into the shadows.

Acknowledgements

Some of these stories have appeared in the following journals, anthologies and broadcasts:

'The Devil's Hand', PJ Quinn, *Pressed by Unseen Feet: An Anthology of Ghostly Writing*, edited by Rose Drew and Alan Gillott, Stairwell Books, 2012

'**Night Call**', *Northern Type 51: An anthology of poetry and prose by writers across Yorkshire and nearby areas,* Northern Co-operative Writers Forum, 2010

'The Dream Machine', *Aireings,* no.6, 1983; *W.E.A. Women's Studies Newsletter,* Issue 3, New Series, May, 1985; broadcast on *Radio Leeds,* March 1984 Inspiration for the novel, *The Keepers*

'**Apple Blossom**' published as 'The Apple Blossom Lady', *Just Beverley*, Issue 60, January 2020

'**Sophie's Choice**' PJ Quinn, Crime Readers' Association website, 2021
https://thecra.co.uk/short_stories/

'**Safe House**', *Just Beverley, YourLocal Link,* Issue 63, March 2020

'**Cavern**', *Pressed by Unseen Feet: An Anthology of Ghostly Writing*, edited by Rose Drew and Alan Gillott, Stairwell Books, 2012

'**The Deadly Morris Dance**', PJ Quinn, *More Exhibitionism: Poems and Prose from the Spoken Word*, ed. Glen Taylor, Stairwell Books, 2016, and the Crime Writers Association website, October 2021 https://thecra.co.uk/short_stories/the-deadly-morris-dance/

'**For the Children**' published in *She*, October 1980

'**Glebe House**', broadcast on *Radio Leeds*, 15.09.87; published in *Joyride: a collection of short stories*, ed. Zoe Rock, New Fiction, 2000

'**The Tennis Girls**' PJ Quinn, Crime Readers' Association website, June 2021 https://thecra.co.uk/short_stories/

'**The Rains**', *Dream Catcher*, Issue 44, 2022

Fighting Cock Press
2 Pinfold Close, Riccall,
York YO19 6QZ

Original Fighting Cock logo by Stanley Chapman.

RRP £10

Printed in Great Britain
by Amazon